MEET THE FORTU

Fortune of the Month: Mad___
Fortunado

Age: 29

Vital Statistics: Blonde and blue-eyed, and prettier than she lets on.

Claim to Fame: Perhaps the most hardworking of the Houston branch of the Fortune family. So why doesn't she ever get what she deserves?

Romantic Prospects: Not looking good. The man who has occupied most of her fantasies for the past five years has now become her greatest rival.

"I've worked my butt off for Fortunado Real Estate forever, knowing that someday the company would be passed down to me. And now my dad has informed me I have to fight for the job that should rightfully be mine. I can't believe he has chosen Zach McCarter, of all people, as his other candidate for the position.

Zach is gorgeous, and driven, and the King of the Flirts. And if I ever had the slightest, tiniest dream of making him mine, my father has effectively squashed it. I can't let Zach win! From now on, I'm all business, all the time. And Zach is The Enemy. But why does my enemy have to be so damn sexy?"

* * *

THE FORTUNES OF TEXAS:
THE RULEBREAKERS:

Making their own rules for love in the Wild West!

Dear Reader,

It's said that beauty is in the eye of the beholder. Yet so often society sets ideals and judges a person's worth based on personal appearance. In *Maddie Fortune's Perfect Man*, book five in the new Fortunes of Texas continuity, the heroine, Maddie Fortune, always thought hard work and dedication would help her get ahead, but she's tested when the one thing she worked for her entire adult life ends up not being the sure thing she thought it would be. She ends up having to dig a little deeper. In the process, she learns about herself and hero Zach McCarter. Zach helps her realize no one can make her feel bad about herself unless she lets them. And she *won't* let them.

I hope you love Maddie and Zach's story as much as I enjoyed writing it. Please link up with me on Facebook at Facebook.com/nrobardsthompson; on Twitter at Twitter.com/nrtwrites; or drop me a line at nrobardsthompson@yahoo.com. I love to hear from readers!

Warmly,

Nancy

Maddie Fortune's Perfect Man

—

Nancy Robards Thompson

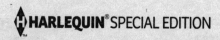
HARLEQUIN® SPECIAL EDITION

Special thanks and acknowledgment to
Nancy Robards Thompson for her contribution to
the Fortunes of Texas: The Rulebreakers continuity.

Recycling programs
for this product may
not exist in your area.

ISBN-13: 978-1-335-46573-3

Maddie Fortune's Perfect Man

Copyright © 2018 by Harlequin Books S.A.

HARLEQUIN®
™ www.Harlequin.com

Printed in U.S.A.

National bestselling author **Nancy Robards Thompson** holds a degree in journalism. She worked as a newspaper reporter until she realized reporting "just the facts" bored her silly. Now that she has much more content to report to her muse, Nancy loves writing women's fiction and romance full-time. Critics have deemed her work "funny, smart and observant." She resides in Florida with her husband and daughter. You can reach her at nancyrobardsthompson.com and Facebook.com/nancyrobardsthompsonbooks.

Books by Nancy Robards Thompson

Harlequin Special Edition

Celebration, TX

The Cowboy Who Got Away
A Bride, a Barn, and a Baby
The Cowboy's Runaway Bride

Celebrations, Inc.

His Texas Christmas Bride
How to Marry a Doctor
A Celebration Christmas
Celebration's Baby
Celebration's Family
Celebration's Bride
Texas Christmas
Texas Magic
Texas Wedding

The Fortunes of Texas: The Secret Fortunes

Fortune's Surprise Engagement

The Fortunes of Texas: Welcome to Horseback Hollow

Falling for Fortune

The Fortunes of Texas: Whirlwind Romance

Fortune's Unexpected Groom

Visit the Author Profile page
at Harlequin.com for more titles.

This book is dedicated to my beloved Samantha, faithful friend, smiling muse and ambassador of all dogs. You stole the heart of this cat lady. Rest in peace, my sweet corgi girl. I'll miss you every day.

Chapter One

Kenneth Fortunado tapped his champagne flute with a table knife. The *ping, ping, ping* of metal on crystal silenced the small gathering of family and friends, whom he'd summoned to the impromptu afternoon barbecue.

Maddie Fortunado shivered as a frisson of anticipation spiraled through her.

A champagne toast at a barbecue. It can only mean one thing.

Finally.

She'd been dreaming of this day.

"Does everyone have a glass of bubbly?" Kenneth asked. "I have a special announcement."

Maddie plucked a flute off the tray of a passing server and turned expectantly toward her father. Catching his eye, she checked her posture and held her glass high. He flashed her a knowing smile and lifted his flute to her in a private *cheers*, before surveying the small crowd he'd gathered on the back terrace of the Fortunado estate.

"Barbara?" he called. "Barbara, where are you? Where is my lovely wife?"

Her mother did indeed look lovely in her powder-blue sweater set, which she'd paired with ivory silk trousers and her signature double strand of pearls. Barbara waved from the back of the terrace where she appeared to be giving the caterer last-minute instructions.

"Barbara, dear," Kenneth said. "Please join me."

Demonstrating that a Southern woman neither rushed nor allowed herself to be rushed, Barbara held up a ladylike index finger, signaling to Kenneth that she'd be there in a moment, and continued her business with the chef.

Maddie allowed her gaze to meander over to her coworker Zach McCarter, who was talking to her sisters, Schuyler and Valene, and Schuyler's fiancé as everyone waited for Kenneth and Barbara to share their big news. Her toes curled in her navy Jack Rogers sandals. Somehow, Zach managed to look masculine—and sexy as hell—holding the delicate crystal champagne glass by the stem, totally oblivious to the fact that she was watching him.

Her uncle Bill, her mom's brother, whom she hadn't seen in months, had come back to Houston for the announcement at their parents' behest, and was engrossed in conversation with Zach and the group. Obviously, her family didn't think there was anything out of the ordinary that Zach had been included in this day of special news.

Zach, who had until a few weeks ago been the broker in charge of Fortunado Real Estate's San Antonio office, had arrived at the house before Maddie, and her mother—as intuitive as ever—had been in the kitchen and had warned her he was here.

"Oh!" Barbara's hand had flown to her mouth, as if she hadn't meant for the exclamation to escape.

"By the way," she'd said, "before you go out there, I thought you should know your father invited Zach Mc-Carter to be here today."

Maddie's stomach had flip-flopped, then plunged. "Here? For the barbecue?"

Barbara grimaced. "Yes. He's out on the porch. Your father insisted on inviting him, even though I said I thought it wasn't a good idea." Barbara shot Maddie a knowing look. "I hope you don't mind."

"Why would I mind?" Maddie kept her voice level and her poker face firmly fixed.

"Why would you mind?" Barbara had shrugged. "Well, I thought this announcement that your father and I are about to make would've been best kept to just family first. But you know how he is. Once he gets something in his head, there's no talking him out of it. It's best just to go with it."

Happy to have the forewarning, she'd seen Zach before she'd opened the French doors that led out to the terrace. In the split instant when her eyes had picked him out of the group that had grown to include more friends than family, her heart had performed a two-step that had caused her to put her hand to her chest.

She looked at Zach standing there, so comfortable in his own skin, laughing with her sisters. The sheer beauty of him—of them all—made the scene look like it could have been an ad for Ralph Lauren or some other all-American line that featured buff, gorgeous people.

Perfection seemed to come so effortlessly to Zach.

This stolen opportunity to drink in his masculine beauty was a smidgen of unadulterated heaven. From the top of his curly blond head—with hair that was on the longish side, but still looked professional—to the bottom of his six-foot-four-inch frame, he was sheer perfection.

His light blue eyes were slightly downturned and adorably crinkled at the edges when he smiled. Maddie took a moment to pay homage to that strong, structured jawline, to those wide shoulders and his impressive height. He was tall, but so was she and next to him, she felt feminine. His nose was just a little crooked and that scar on his chin that she couldn't see but could visualize were just enough to lend a masculine edge to his classic features. Good thing, too, because with his sun-kissed honey-blond hair, perfected by his convertible BMW, he could easily have been too pretty. But he wasn't. He was perfect.

She watched Schuyler reach up and ruffle Zach's hair. She'd wager that she was telling him that people paid big bucks for highlights like that. Schuyler was always bemoaning the high price of beauty when she migrated back to Houston from Austin every six weeks for hair appointments. That was precisely why Maddie preferred to keep her blond hair natural. She didn't have time to get roped into regular salon appointments for upkeep. The mere thought of the obligation gave her hives.

On a better note, she wished she could freeze this stolen moment and savor it over and over. Because Zach looked particularly gorgeous on this fine Sunday afternoon. There was something especially enticing about the way his light blue eyes crinkled as he laughed at something Schuyler was saying. He was probably humoring her as she went on and on about his highlights. He looked so comfortable in his own sexy skin. He was mesmerizing, and the sight of him sent a quiver down to the pit of her stomach. Maddie fisted her free hand, the one that wasn't holding her champagne, so tightly her nails dug into her palms.

Oh, Zach, you sexy thing.

A wisp of wistful regret skittered through Maddie as she realized he would never be anything more to her than a fantasy. He couldn't even be her secret crush anymore, which had been so easy when he was at the San Antonio office. She'd had a chance to get to know him better since he'd transferred to Houston. But she needed to rein it in if she was going to be his boss, which was about to happen once her father made the big announcement.

Any second now.

But until then, she was free to indulge one last tiny little daydream—

Uh-oh—

She froze as Zach's gaze locked with hers. It happened so fast and the jolt was so gripping, she couldn't look away. It was just as well. In her peripheral vision, she could see that Val was talking to Uncle Bill and Schuyler was talking to her fiancé, Carlo Mendoza, leaving poor Zach unentertained. If she looked away too fast, he might think she hadn't wanted him to catch her watching him. Even though she *hadn't* intended for him to catch her looking. It was best to hold up her end of the subtly flirtatious stare-down, which she did— brilliantly, if she did say so herself—dropping her gaze to her champagne flute for a single beat and then snaring his gaze again.

It was a silent dare to see who would look away first.

She sighed inwardly.

It's been fun, Zach, but now it's time for me to move on.

That's what she was telegraphing to him. He didn't seem to be receiving the message, because if he had, surely, he would've had the good grace to look away.

Instead, he raised his hand to her. She made the same motion in return.

In the end, neither of them lost the challenge because her father called it a draw when he started talking and broke the spell. They both gave him their attention. Her mother was now standing at Kenneth's side and he handed her a glass of champagne.

"My family—" Kenneth gestured toward Maddie and then toward her sisters. "Madeleine, Valene, Schuyler and Carlo. And Zach. Zach, I include you because you are like a son to Barbara and me—like family to all of us."

Family? Maddie blanched. *No. That would make him my brother.*

Of course, Zach had been over to the Fortunado homestead. Since he didn't have family in town, they'd invited him last Thanksgiving.

She'd never think of Zach as a brother. Not with the fantasies she had of him.

Those fantasies were anything but sisterly...

"Speaking of sons," Kenneth continued. "I wish Everett, Connor and Gavin could be here today." Kenneth's gaze scanned the group of well-wishers. "Everett and Lila are away on their honeymoon. Those crazy kids eloped after they saw everything that's involved in putting together a wedding. It's not too late to follow suit, Carlo." Everyone laughed. Schuyler held on tight to Carlo and shook her head as Kenneth continued. "Connor and Gavin couldn't get away since they're coming for Schuyler and Carlo's wedding at the end of the month. But—"

Kenneth stopped and shook his head. A slow smile tipped up the corners of his mouth. "I am a lucky man to be surrounded by so much love." He lifted his glass to Schuyler and Carlo. "To my lovely daughter and her husband-to-be and to all of you. Thank you so much for being here this afternoon. It was a last-minute invitation, but as I told you, it's important to Barbara and me to share our news with you first. You are important to us and we wanted you to hear it first."

Kenneth's smile faded.

"When my mother passed away, it was a wake-up call. Those of you who knew Starlight know she was larger than life. She lived every day to the fullest. Her passing not only gave me pause, it made me stop and take inventory of my life. That inventory revealed that I have a lot of lost time to make up for." He put his arm around Barbara. "Not only that, but our children are all grown. They're getting married and leaving the nest. It's made Barb and me realize we have a lot of living to do. It's time for *us*. However, it's difficult to make time for us when I'm working eighty-hour weeks." He paused and smiled down at Barbara. "Thank you for being patient with me, love."

Barbara kissed his cheek.

"With that in mind," Kenneth said, "I am so pleased to announce that right after Schuyler and Carlo's wedding, I will retire from Fortunado Real Estate."

Even though they were exactly the words Maddie had been expecting, a gasp escaped her throat as she led the gathering in a round of applause, sloshing a little champagne as she clapped.

Barbara held up her hand to silence them. "And I am pleased to announce that right after the big wedding, Kenneth and I will take a second honeymoon. We will be leaving on a four-month cruise around the world. Forty-nine ports of call—thirty-two countries on six continents."

More applause.

Maddie's chest hurt and she realized she'd been holding her breath. She was thrilled for her parents, but she was waiting for the *next part*. The part of the announcement where her father said that he was promoting her, that she would be stepping up as his successor to lead Fortunado Real Estate into the next chapter.

"I booked the cruise and told him the ship would sail on June fourth—with or without him," Barbara said. "I told him I'd be on that boat and I hoped he would be there, too. Because even with all this life inventory, we all know that's the only way I'd ever get him to finally make the leap into retirement."

Maddie inhaled sharply to quell her impatience.

"Now, now, my love," Kenneth said.

Maddie blew out all the air from her lungs. Her heart thudded. She could hear her blood rushing in her ears. Her father put his arm around her mother and lovingly massaged her neck, which made Barbara squirm and swat him away. She'd never been one for public displays of affection.

"Kenneth, not in front of the kids," Barbara said.

Yes, not in front of the kids, Dad. Yuck. Save it for the cruise and get to the rest of the announcement.

Kenneth and Barbara raised their glasses to the small crowd.

"Thank you for helping us celebrate our big decision."

Everyone raised their glasses in return and offered cheers and good words like *congratulations*, *hear! hear!*, *to your health and happiness* and *bon voyage*.

But wait... What about the rest... What about the announcement of your successor?

Maddie battled the demons of disappointment as she watched her sisters rush to congratulate their parents with hugs and squeals. She blinked once, twice. Took one more slow, deep breath, doing her best to slay the monster inside.

Okay. So, he wasn't going to announce her promotion now.

It was okay. Really, it was.

She blinked again and reframed. It wasn't that big of a deal that her father hadn't yet announced that she would be his successor.

Maddie let the words ruminate in her brain for a moment.

This afternoon was for her parents. It was a big, big deal for them. It was a huge step for them. Today was about them.

Not her.

Them.

Her cheeks burned as she knocked back the rest of her champagne, draining the half-full glass. She could let them have their day. She *should* let them have their day. Her dad probably wanted to talk to her privately before he made the announcement.

Of course. He wouldn't just announce her promotion without preparing her first.

Today was a day to celebrate Kenneth and Barbara. In fact, she was proud of her dad for not making today all about business. It took a lot of restraint on his part, since he was always all business, all the time. Plus, something so important as her stepping into her father's shoes needed to be discussed. Even though they had already discussed it—in broad terms. But now that his retirement had a fixed date, they would need to discuss her salary. They needed to talk about his expectations. She needed to make sure he understood she wanted complete control. His role would be as support system to her.

Or better yet, he'd stay out of Fortunado Real Estate altogether and enjoy his retirement as she implemented her vision for the company.

Her gaze found Zach again. Like her, he stood just outside of the knot of people clustered around her parents, wishing them well.

Once she took over, she would offer Zach a lovely promotion. It was the least she could do if she couldn't offer him her body— *Stop that.* To date, she'd never offered him her body and now she never would. And that was not the way a boss should think about an employee. Even if said employee was drop-dead gorgeous and flirted outrageously with her. He flirted outrageously with all women. He had a different girl with him every time she saw him. And that's why she needed to focus on what would come next: her promotion. It was a chance to give her all to something bigger than herself—something that would never let her down. That was the way to go.

She would always love Zach, but he would never know it.

That was the price she would pay to secure her future. A future so close she could taste it.

Zach McCarter was honored to be invited to hear his boss's big announcement. From the first minute Zach had joined the Fortunado Real Estate team five years ago, Kenneth Fortunado had made him feel like part of the family. Even so, he felt a little out of place here today. Like a fish out of water among Kenneth's adult children and close friends. However, when his boss welcomed him as part of the family, it would be rude—hell, it would be downright ungrateful—to second-guess the invitation.

His gaze landed on Maddie Fortunado, who was standing apart from her sisters and the others who were clustered around their parents. Only he and Maddie, with her long blond hair and perfect skin, hung back.

She stood with her arms folded, wearing a *Mona Lisa* smile that didn't quite reach her blue eyes. Zach knew she would wait until the scrum had dissipated before going in. He knew this because it's what he'd do. He and Maddie were a lot alike when it came to things like this—and in their approach to business. But their backgrounds were polar opposite.

With her Ivy League education and continental upbringing, Maddie Fortunado was not your standard Texas debutante. She was smart—too smart to concern herself with inconsequential things that didn't matter. She put her Harvard Business School education to good use at Fortunado Real Estate and seemed to live, eat, breathe and sleep her career.

While he and Maddie were philosophically alike, Zach hadn't been born into money. He wasn't implying that Maddie didn't work hard. In fact, he had to hand it to her, she never coasted on the privilege of being the boss's daughter. She was good at her job as vice president of sales. She was always in the office. Every time he was there, so was she. No one could accuse her of not pulling her weight. But at the end of the day, she was the boss's daughter. That's why he had to check any feelings that might have remotely resembled attraction.

And there had been a few.

Zach had worked double time just to get to the starting gate of his career, so that a man like Kenneth Fortunado not only knew his name, but respected him enough to invite him into his home and include him in an occasion like this.

Maddie glanced his way again and he made a face at her. She smiled—as he knew she would. She shook her head and rolled her eyes good-naturedly.

Zach closed the distance between them, walking across the marble back porch, past the koi pond to stand next to her.

"Hey," he said.

"Hey, yourself." She cocked a brow. "I guess they let anyone in here these days."

"Surprised by the announcement?" he asked.

She shrugged. "In some ways, yes, but it's been a long time coming. So, in that regard, no."

"What happens next?" he asked.

"What do you mean?" She raised her chin a fraction of an inch, a tell that she knew something she wasn't sharing.

"If anyone knows what's going to happen with the business after your father retires, it would be you."

She opened her blue eyes wide, obviously feigning cluelessness, but she wasn't very good at it.

"I don't know, Zach. I guess you'll just have to wait for another Fortunado family announcement."

She fisted her hands on her hips and the movement showed off her sleek tanned arms beneath her crisp white sleeveless blouse. She had great arms that were toned and feminine. And long, long legs that could drive a man to distraction if he allowed it. Zach wouldn't allow it. He couldn't allow it, he thought, forbidding himself to glance down.

It was likely that Maddie would be named her father's successor. That meant she would go from being the boss's daughter to being the boss. No matter how alluring he found those long legs, they weren't worth compromising his job. He'd worked too hard to get to where he was today to risk losing it all.

"Everyone, lunch is ready," said Barbara. The crowd around her and Kenneth thinned. "Please help yourselves. We have pulled pork, barbecued brisket, and chicken. I hope you brought your appetites. Because there's plenty of food and I don't want any leftovers."

Schuyler and Carlo were the first ones to approach the buffet. Zach and Maddie continued to hang back and let the other guests and Fortunado siblings go first. No matter how many family functions or Sunday lunches like this one that he'd attended, he always tried to err on the side of politeness. He was thirty-two years old and had been in the business since he was eighteen, but at times like this, he still felt out of place. If he thought about it too hard, the fifteen-year-old boy who was on the outside looking in beckoned him farther back into the periphery, where he would feel more comfortable watching than diving into the middle of everything. He'd outgrown his insecurities, of course. He'd like to think he'd gotten as strong as he was to spite them. Because confidence had been a must to succeed in the real estate business. In fact, in this industry, confidence was everything. But being in the Fortunado home like this, he preferred to stand back and watch the family dynamics. Watch and learn. The natural family rhythm fascinated him. Especially families like this that were so different from what he was used to.

"The food doesn't get any warmer," said Maddie. "You better get it while it's hot. Or at least before my cousin Dale goes through the line."

Maddie nodded toward a tall skinny guy who was still talking to Kenneth.

"He didn't earn the name *the closer* because he's good at sales," Maddie said. "He eats a lot."

"The closer, huh?" Zach said. "That sounds formidable."

"Don't say I didn't warn you."

Maddie motioned for him to join her as she approached the buffet line. He followed. She picked up two plates and offered him one. Her hand brushed his as he accepted it.

"Are you happy at Fortunado, Zach?" she asked.

The non sequitur made him do a mental double take. "Happy?" he repeated. "Of course I'm happy."

"Good to know." Her gaze searched his eyes. There was something in them he didn't understand. Especially when they dipped to his lips for the briefest of seconds.

She bit her bottom lip, a hint of color blossoming in her cheeks, before lifting her eyes to hold his gaze again.

There was something understatedly sexy about her and the realization caught him off guard. He could test these mixed signals she was sending—these cracks in her buttoned-up, businesslike armor that kept him guessing, making him wonder if he was reading her right. And he was usually very good at reading people. He prided himself on it.

But these flirty looks of Maddie's sometimes morphed into stare-downs that became games of chicken to see who would look away first. The accidental brush of hands, and now asking him if he was happy at Fortunado? What was that all about?

"Why?" he asked. "If I was, say, restless, would you be willing to make it worth my while to stay?"

"And how would you propose I make it worth your while?"

She watched him, waiting for his answer as she held out the white china plate for the server to dish up a piece of chicken and a portion of brisket.

He arched a brow, and his gut clenched at the thoughts swirling around his head. He felt as if he were contemplating taking something that didn't belong to him. Like finding a twenty-dollar bill on the sidewalk—you could stuff it in your pocket and walk away…or you could do the right thing and try to find the owner.

She must've read it in his expression.

"You're full of yourself, McCarter." He watched her walk to an empty table off to the side, rather than joining her sisters and Carlo at the one in the middle of the patio.

Zach took his plate of barbecue and followed her, claiming the seat next to her. "Full of myself? That wasn't a very nice thing to say."

Her eyes widened. "You're so sensitive."

"That's me. I'm just a sensitive kind of guy. Isn't that what the ladies want? A sensitive guy?"

She cut a piece of chicken off the bone. Raising the fork to her lips, she stopped short of putting the bite into her mouth, a mischievous smile tipping up the corners of her lips.

"Is that what you tell all the ladies?" Maddie asked. "That you're a sensitive kind of guy?"

Zach flashed his best smile. "Whatever works."

"Whatever works," she repeated. "Is that your philosophy?"

"Nope. Sensitivity is my philosophy. How could you forget?" He made a stabbing gesture in the center of his chest. "I thought we'd finally found something in common. You know, you liking sensitive men and me being sensitive."

She laughed and her cheeks colored. He liked the thought of rattling calm, cool, collected, perfect Madeleine Fortunado. He wanted to get under her skin. Because it was the closest he'd come to ever getting under anything of hers.

Maddie took a sip of her margarita, willing herself to calm down. She was grateful when Schuyler and Carlo moved from their original spot and joined them.

"What's wrong?" Schuyler asked Maddie when they sat down. "What did I miss?"

Zach snared Maddie's gaze and he raised his eyebrow, issuing a challenge for her to explain the conversation.

"Zach will explain." She turned to him and smiled.

"Whatever works." He winked at her and her cheeks colored again.

He cleared his throat. "I was just asking Maddie what she did for fun. You know, I'm starting to get the feeling that all she does is work. She doesn't always work, does she?"

"Pretty much," Schuyler said.

"There has to be something else," he said. "I'm curious about what she likes to do for fun."

Schuyler looked as if she wasn't buying it. "Oh, really? I know my sister works a lot, but you two get together every Friday night at the Thirsty Ox, don't you?"

"Of course we do," Maddie said.

"But that's still work-related," Zach qualified.

"And Zach usually brings a date," Maddie added. "Or he stops by and rushes out to meet a date."

"I didn't realize you noticed," Zach said.

Carlo and Schuyler watched them banter back and forth as if they were the lunchtime entertainment, and Maddie wanted to bolt.

"Even so," he said. "How is it that I don't know much about you? What are your interests outside of the office? When you're not thinking about real estate, what do you think about?"

Maddie felt herself blanch. "That's a little personal, don't you think?"

"No, it's not," Zach said. "Is it? I don't mean to make you uncomfortable. I just want to know you better. I was hoping you would tell me one thing I didn't know." He held up his hands. "But if you'd rather not, it's okay."

Before Maddie could reply, he turned his attention to Carlo and Schuyler.

"Where will you live after you're married?" he asked.

"I'm helping them find a house in Austin," Maddie cut in before her sister could answer. "And I have a dog."

"What?" Zach looked puzzled.

"You asked me to tell you one thing about myself that you didn't know. I have a dog. So, there you go. That's one thing."

Zach nodded. "I didn't know that. Thank you for sharing it with me. What kind of dog?"

Maddie shook her head. "Nope. You said one thing. Now it's your turn. One thing. Start talking, McCarter."

He blinked. "Fair enough. I lived in San Antonio for five years and before that I traveled around a lot."

"I know that about you," Maddie said. "Tell me something I don't know."

"Really?" He wrinkled his brow. "How do you know that?"

Maddie bit the insides of her cheeks. She had to be careful not to tip her hand. A lot of her Zach information had come from perusing his social media accounts, which were usually pretty generic and real estate–oriented, but occasionally a friend of his would post a personal morsel and Maddie would gobble it up like cake. Of course, she'd be mortified if he ever found out that she stalked him on Facebook and Instagram. But, hey, it was a free country, and his social media pages were open to the public. It wasn't as if she'd hacked in or was doing anything devious. It was all completely aboveboard.

Sort of.

Social media was a secret crush resource. It was fair game.

Even so, she would be mortified if he found out.

"I'm sure you mentioned it before," she said nonchalantly. "How else would I know?"

"Is that a tactic to get me to divulge two things about myself to your one?" He looked smug, as if he'd uncovered her diabolical plan.

"Okay. Whatever." Maddie shrugged him off, wanting to quit while she was ahead. "It's not that important."

She immediately regretted how cold her words sounded. If she was good at flirting, she could've gotten some mileage out of their banter. But the truth was, flirting sort of freaked her out. She could do it up to a point, but when he got too close, she choked. When she choked, her defense mechanisms kicked in and she came across as prickly. Because it was so much easier to pretend like she didn't care. It was just as well, she supposed. Because she *shouldn't* care.

But then Zach was sitting there pretending to look wounded and her stomach flipped.

"Ouch!" he said. "I have been put in my place."

No! That's not what I meant. I didn't know what else to say.

Then he smiled and those dimples winked at her. If

her mind had been spinning before, she was at a total loss for words now.

She was glad when his phone rang.

He took it out of his pocket and glanced at the screen. "Sorry, I need to take this call. Excuse me, please?"

She watched him unfold his long body from his place at the table. He answered the call while he was still close enough for Maddie to hear him say, "Hey, how are you?" His voice sounded low and sexy, qualities that suggested he wasn't talking to a client. Her heart fluttered and then sank. She'd heard him on the phone with clients before. This was definitely a girlfriend. Zach had a lot of girlfriends because he was a flirt. He had an easy appeal, especially with women. He flirted with any woman who would flirt back... Not so unlike the way he was flirting with her.

You're not special. He flirts with everyone.

That thought was like a cold glass of water, a reality check to remind herself that she really should stop this nonsense before she embarrassed herself. She was already way out of her element carrying on like she had been.

He was good at what he did. And because he was good at what he did, Maddie needed him on her team at Fortunado Real Estate when she took over for her father.

Priorities. Do not muddy the waters. Remember what's important.

"Speaking of house hunting," Maddie said, looking at her sister.

Schuyler looked puzzled. "We weren't."

"I mentioned it a few minutes ago," Maddie said.

"I have a house to show you. It's not even on the market yet. One of my clients gave me the heads-up. It's a dream house so it'll go fast. When can we go look?"

Schuyler clapped her hands. "Let's go this week. As soon as you can come to Austin." She turned and looked at her husband-to-be. "Carlo, can you take some time off next week?"

"Anything for you, my love." Carlo leaned in and planted a kiss on Schuyler's cheek.

"Okay, then," Maddie said. "I'll call my client and check her availability."

She started to excuse herself from the table, but Zach was already making his way back.

On second thought, maybe the call to the client could wait until after lunch.

Zach caught her eye as he walked back to the table. His long stride was loose and comfortable. Her mind raced, searching for something witty to say after he sat down. She thought about quipping about the call being personal, maybe teasing him about showing his sensitive side. But they'd worn out that joke. Instead, she resorted to the traditional and polite.

"Is everything okay?"

"Sure," he said. "But I do need to go."

Maddie's heart sank.

"But before I go, I want to thank your parents and congratulate them on your father's big decision. But first, Ping-Pong."

Maddie was sure she'd heard him wrong. "Did you say Ping-Pong?"

He flashed that grin and those dimples made Maddie's toes curl in her sandals.

"It was my favorite pastime when I was nine," he said. "I'm sure you didn't know that."

She laughed. *Ping-Pong.*

"No, I didn't know that."

"Do you play?"

"As a matter of fact, I was pretty darn good at it, back in the day."

"We should play sometime," he said.

Maddie drew in a sharp breath and nearly choked. She didn't understand her reaction. He wasn't asking her on a date.

"You two should *totally* play," Schuyler urged. "In fact, I think we still have a Ping-Pong table somewhere around here. Mom never gets rid of anything. She just learns new techniques to masterfully store everything. But I digress. We should have a Ping-Pong date night. It would be so much fun. Totally retro. My money would be on Mads, though. She was pretty good at it. Or at least she was the most competitive out of all of us. She's always hated to lose. She still does."

Maddie impaled her sister with a look, to which Schuyler seemed oblivious.

Not true! Okay, maybe it's a little true.

Even so, she wished Schuyler hadn't said it.

"It's a date, then," Zach said. "The loser will buy the winner's beer one Friday at the Thirsty Ox." He turned and started walking away, but stopped and turned back. "And the loser has to tell the other winner five personal things."

Chapter Two

The next morning, Maddie glanced up from her computer and saw her sister Valene standing in the doorway of her office.

"Do you have a moment?" Val asked. "I have some questions about the McKinney listing on West Pine."

Maddie's eyes flitted to the time at the bottom of her computer screen. When she'd gotten to her desk at 7:30 this morning, her father's executive assistant, Rae Rowley, had phoned and asked her to clear her schedule at 11:00. Maddie had been a jumble of nerves for more than three hours this morning, doing everything she could to distract herself. Why hadn't Val come to her sooner?

The 11:00 meeting was *the meeting*. The one she'd

been waiting for since she'd joined the firm. Probably longer than that—since she was born.

She'd been reading an email about a career day event sponsored by the local school system. She'd volunteered to share everything she knew and loved about the real estate business with elementary schoolkids, but today she was reading the material to distract herself more so than to prepare for the annual event, which was next month.

The diversion had worked because now it was 10:55.

"I'm supposed to meet with Dad in five minutes." She smiled a knowing smile and her younger sister's mouth fell open as realization dawned in her eyes.

"Is this about…?" Val made circles with her hands, as if she were indicating something that was too big to put into words.

"I think so," Maddie said. "I hope so. I guess I'll find out in about—" She glanced at the time again. "Four minutes."

Maddie stood and gathered her leather folio and her lucky Montblanc fountain pen. It had been a gift from her father when he'd promoted her to vice president.

"I'm sorry I can't talk right now. Unless it's super quick and you want to walk and talk. Or we could meet later?"

"Oh, my gosh, don't you worry one bit." Val reached out and gave Maddie's arm a little squeeze. "My questions can wait. This is much more important. This…" She made the all-encompassing hand circles again. "This is our future. Fortunado Real Estate's future.

And I am thrilled that I know about your promotion before anyone else."

Maddie shrugged. "It isn't official just yet."

"We all know it's coming." Valene pulled Maddie into a hug. "Okay, chief. Go in there and show him who's boss."

Val let go and grimaced, shaking her head as if trying to erase the words. "Well, you probably don't need to show Dad you're the boss. He already knows. Oh, you know what I mean."

Sweet Val. She was young and a little naive, but her heart was in the right place and she had such good instincts. It would be a great morale booster for her if Maddie could find some way to reward her—maybe a token promotion—after things settled down. Maddie filed that thought away to revisit soon. Right now, she had a meeting to attend.

She and Val chatted as they walked down the office's main hall toward the formidable double doors at the end of the passageway.

"The long and short of it is the McKinneys and I are wrangling on the listing price for their house," Val said. "They think we should ask $200,000 more than what I'm recommending for the property."

"Did you base the price on comps in the area?" Maddie asked.

Valene shrugged. "Really, there's nothing quite like it in the neighborhood. That's why I need your advice. They say their home is special—"

"Everyone thinks their home is special," Maddie said. "And I'm sure it is, to them. But at that price, we're edging close to $185 per square foot. It would be a record for that neighborhood."

By that time, they'd reached their dad's office and his assistant spoke before Val could. "Your father is expecting you, Ms. Fortunado. Please go in when you're ready."

"Thank you, Rae," Maddie said and turned her attention back to Val. "I'm sure they don't want to price themselves out of the market. I'll stop by your desk after I'm finished and we can figure it out. But I need to go. I don't want to be late."

She hated to leave Valene hanging, but of all people, Val knew it wasn't a good idea to keep their father waiting. Especially not today. Besides, this was a good exercise for Val. If she was going to succeed, and Maddie had all the confidence in the world that she would, her sister needed to learn how to steer the client toward a reasonable listing price. It took practice, but she'd get the hang of it.

"No, you certainly don't want to keep him waiting." Val said the words with a lilting songlike quality. "Not today. Not for this meeting. Good luck."

Maddie breathed through a hitch of anticipation that had become almost Pavlovian since her father had allowed himself to introduce the *R* word into his vocabulary.

Retirement.

He'd committed to it yesterday when he'd made the big announcement. Now he was about to seal the deal by putting the rest of the plan in place.

Lately, her parents had been talking about spending

more time together. They wanted to travel; her father had been promising he would cut his hours. But even after the barbecue, when he hadn't named Maddie as his successor, she wondered if he'd really go through with it. Something felt a little off. One step at a time, she'd reminded herself last night as she'd tossed and turned while reliving the announcement.

She'd never seen her mother as serious as she'd been when she'd said the cruise around the world would sail with or without him. Barbara didn't draw lines in the sand very often, but when she did, she didn't play. That boat was leaving on June 4, and she would be on it with or without him.

Barbara Fortunado was possibly the only thing Kenneth loved more than Fortunado Real Estate. Sure, he loved his kids, but he'd go insane if his wife was away for four months. Still, he was an all-or-nothing man. There would be no semiretirement for him. There was no way he could stay away from the office that long without making a clean break.

Even if he had sealed the deal on his retirement yesterday, this meeting made the slim chance that he might change his mind seem less likely.

"Are you free for lunch?" Val asked. "We could talk about it then."

Maddie glanced at her watch. It was edging on 11:00. Even if Rae hadn't specifically mentioned lunch when she'd called about the meeting, she'd said *clear your schedule*.

"I'm not sure, Val. You know how Dad is. He may

just want to meet, but he may want to go to lunch afterward."

To celebrate.

Her stomach did a triple gainer at the thought.

Finally.

She would insist they get a bottle of champagne. The very best vintage in the cellar. And when he reminded her it was the middle of the day, that they had work to do, she would put her hand on his arm and tell him that he had earned this champagne. It was as much to celebrate his life-changing decision as to celebrate her promotion.

She'd pick up the tab. It would be symbolic of his passing the mantle.

"I don't have anything scheduled this afternoon," Val said. "Let me know when you're free. I'd really like to get back to the McKinneys before the end of the day."

"Of course. Of course." Maddie smiled her most benevolent smile. "I'll see you as soon as I'm free."

After all, Val was Maddie's protégé. Just as their father had trained her, it was up to her to pay it forward and teach Valene everything she knew about the Houston real estate market. Since they were so close in age, it was unlikely that Val would ever head up Fortunado. After all, the company only had room for one president. But Maddie would make sure that Val's hard work was rewarded.

Once Val got more experience, maybe Maddie could make her a vice president? Or CFO?

Val nodded. "Sounds good. Thanks, Maddie. Good luck." She mouthed the words *and congratulations.*

As Maddie turned, she smiled at Rae and walked toward her father's office. All the hard work she'd poured into her job was about to pay off. All the long days and weekends dedicated to business rather than dating and having fun. No, scratch that. Work was fun. It was a sure thing, a solid investment. The harder she worked, the more she proved herself.

She didn't mind chasing after a business deal. In fact, she was in her glory when she was hunting down a deal. She'd latch onto it and stay the fight until she won. But she never chased men. Men were untrustworthy. They were too unpredictable. Giving her all to business was the closest thing to a sure thing she'd ever find.

Work was a solid investment of her time. Unlike the uncertainty of the dating world. Would she like to get married and have a family? Sure. Someday. But right now, Fortunado Real Estate claimed her full attention. The more she proved herself, the more comfortable her father seemed to be about retiring and turning Fortunado Real Estate over to her.

The sound of male voices coming from her father's office snapped her out of her reverie before she gave a staccato rap on his office door.

"Enter," Kenneth said.

When she opened the door, she smiled askance when she saw Zach McCarter sitting in one of the two cordovan leather club chairs across from her father's mahogany desk.

Her father and Zach stood up when they saw her.

"I'm sorry." Maddie glanced at her watch to make sure she had the time right. It was 11:01. "I didn't mean to interrupt. Rae said you were ready to meet with me. I can wait outside while you two finish up."

"No," her father said. "Come in. Come in. Zach is part of this meeting, too. Now that we're all here we can begin."

Maddie's stomach dropped as the men lowered themselves into their seats. Why was Zach part of this meeting? This meeting had nothing to do with Zach.

"Sit down, Maddie." Kenneth Fortunado gestured to the matching leather chair next to Zach.

Her mind raced as she smoothed her black pencil skirt before sitting down.

Maybe today isn't the day. And that's okay. It's fine.

Actually, it wasn't okay, but what other option did she have?

She'd talk to her dad after the meeting and assure him she knew it was hard to relinquish control. After all, if anyone knew that, she did. She'd inherited the tendency to micromanage from the man himself. He probably just needed a little reassurance that Fortunado Real Estate would be fine in her hands. It would be more than fine. It would thrive.

He just needed to bite the bullet and make the decision already.

She tamped down her disappointment by letting her gaze do a quick sweep of Zach in his dress khakis and white button-down, which was open at the collar. As always, he looked effortlessly professional. And gorgeous. Neither too casual nor overly preened. Leave it to him and his broad shoulders and perfect butt to make simple white and beige look like a work of art.

Yes, she'd noticed.

She studied the angle of his cheekbones, the slant of his aquiline nose, the waves of his blond hair and the gleam of his blue, blue bedroom eyes. It was hard not to notice Zach McCarter and all his masculine perfection.

In fact, just last night she'd indulged in a late-night fantasy about Zach's *masculine perfection*—those perfect shoulders and butt. And those dimples. Oh, those dimples.

He was gorgeous. And she was human. And he was totally and completely off-limits, which made him the perfect secret crush. And, well, a guy like Zach never looked at a woman like Maddie, which was fine with her. In fact, it was just the way she liked it. If she was going to be his boss, he could never know about the thoughts that ran through her head.

It wasn't as if he was a mind reader. So, she had nothing to worry about.

Except she was worrying about his presence at this meeting. What was he doing here?

Maddie thought her father would've talked to her separately.

A sinking feeling lodged itself in the pit of her stomach.

Last year, Zach had barely edged out Maddie as Fortunado's top sales producer. This year they were running neck and neck. But it was only May and she fully intended to reclaim the throne. That victory would be the final jewel in the crown after she took over for her father. Of course, she'd been focusing on administrative tasks other than sales—mentoring Valene, learning the advertising and promo end of the business, researching client-building methods, and such. There were only so many hours in the day. She was doing all the extras and almost matching Zach as the top sales producer. It went without saying that if all she did was focus on sales, like Zach did, she'd be running circles around McCarter.

"Thank you for making time to meet with me this morning," her father said, as if either of them would've opted out. "I've been eyeing retirement for a while now. It's taken me a long time to wrap my head around the concept, but with a little help from Barbara, I've finally decided to take the plunge."

He paused for what seemed an eternity and Maddie held perfectly still, resisting the urge to shift in her seat, redistributing her impatience.

Now that sinking feeling was gripping her stomach and attempting to turn it inside out.

"Congratulations, Kenneth," Zach said. "I know it wasn't an easy decision."

"Thank you, Zach. It's been one of the most difficult decisions of my life. This business represents the sum of my life's work. I've invested a lot of sweat equity in this place, building it from the ground up. So, you can imagine that I want to leave the business in the best hands once I step back."

Maddie sensed what was about to happen before her father spelled it out. She wanted to say something, but she didn't want Zach McCarter to glimpse any weakness or uncertainty in her. This was *her* future. *Her* legacy. This wasn't happening—

"I consider the two of you my right-hand people,"

Kenneth continued as Maddie's peripheral vision was overtaken by a white-tinged fog.

You can only have one right hand, Dad. Who is it? Him or me? It's me, dammit. It's me. Why are you doing this?

Her gaze could've singed a hole into her father as she tried in vain to telegraph her feelings to him. But he seemed clueless.

"That's why I've narrowed the candidates for my replacement down to the two of you."

He glanced first at Zach and then at Maddie.

"Maddie?" Kenneth's smile fell. "Are you okay?"

Feeling two sets of eyes on her, Maddie forced her mouth into a smile. "I'm just surprised, Dad. This was the last thing I expected when you asked me to meet with you this morning."

Her father gazed at her a few beats too long and she was sure he sensed her confusion. He was an intuitive man. He had to know that this was not just a surprise, but a personal affront, an insult.

"I thought you would've had some kind of idea," her father said, "since we've discussed the possibility of you running Fortunado in the future."

The possibility.

He'd led her to believe that it was more than just a *possibility.* No, he'd led her to believe that she would step into the position of president of Fortunado Real Estate upon his retirement. Now he couldn't walk it back fast enough.

"I guess I thought you were offering more than a *possibility,*" she said.

She had dedicated every bit of her postgraduate self to Fortunado Real Estate. She'd sacrificed her personal life, her dating life, working eighteen-hour days and weekends, making herself available to clients twenty-four hours a day, seven days a week. While her father may not have out-and-out promised her she would be his successor, he had implied it. Besides, Kenneth Fortunado was all about family. Why in the world would he consider turning over the family business to an outsider?

Her father either chose to ignore her remark or pretend as if he hadn't heard it, because he was already moving on. It was a good thing he hadn't pressed her because she wasn't about to say anything more in front of Zach.

Her father leaned forward, his hands folded on his desk. "Barbara and I leave on our cruise on June 4. That means right after the wedding—in approximately two weeks—I will name my successor. If the two of you choose to accept the challenge, one of you will take my place as president of Fortunado Real Estate."

Maddie glanced at Zach, fully expecting him to do the right thing and bow out. She wanted him to hold up his hands and say that it wasn't appropriate, that it wasn't his place to challenge Maddie for what was rightfully hers. Instead, he flashed that perfect smile with those dimples that opened doors and broke hearts. He looked Maddie square in the eyes and said, "I'm in."

His smile was reminiscent of the one he'd given her last night when he'd challenged her to a friendly game of

Ping-Pong. But this was a competition to determine her future—to decide who got control over her birthright.

But damned if her own traitorous heart didn't twist at the sheer rakish beauty of him. That hurt almost as much as the thought of her uncertain future.

"Bring it on," she said, instantly wishing she would've said something a little classier. But he didn't seem to mind. His eyes glinted as if sparked by the competition. She forced her gaze away from the seductive pull of his.

Once upon a time Zach McCarter might have been her secret crush, but now *he* was the competition. As far as she was concerned, he was the enemy.

"Good," said Kenneth, turning his gaze on Maddie. "Maddie, I'm proud of you for rising to the occasion. I must admit that I was worried about how you'd take it. But I have to hand it to you for wanting what's best for the business."

Maddie dug her nails into her palms as she kept the smile fixed on her face. So, he'd worried about how she'd take it, but he hadn't given her the courtesy of a heads-up before this meeting? Oh, yeah, they'd talk about what was best for the *family business* later.

"The real estate business is brutal," said Kenneth. "Whoever takes over Fortunado will likely face much tougher challenges in the years ahead. I want to make sure whoever I choose is up for the long haul."

Ostensibly, he was speaking to both of them, but he was looking at Maddie.

And she'd believed it couldn't possibly get worse.

Were they really going to do this now?

"I'm up for the challenge, Dad." Her voice was clear and her words were crisp. "I didn't realize our family business was up for grabs. You know, open to an outsider."

She was well aware that her words had surpassed crisp and veered into clipped. Her father winced, but she didn't know how Zach reacted because she didn't look at him. But she'd guess that he'd managed to keep a pleasantly stoic poker face. And if she knew what was good for her, she'd compose herself, too.

Her father cleared his throat. "The business is not up for grabs, as you put it. You might be the one I choose if you prove yourself the worthiest."

Prove myself the worthiest? What the hell do you think I've been trying to do my entire adult life?

Her father's words shook her to her very core. After all the hours she'd put in, all the sacrifices she'd made for the good of the company, he still wasn't satisfied that she'd proven herself worthy?

If she didn't know better, she might think that this had more to do with turning over the reins to one of his daughters. His sons weren't interested. So, what did he do? He *adopted* one.

At least she had the good sense to not talk about this now. But they would talk. He had better believe they would talk.

Even in her fury, she had the presence of mind to know that her father wasn't a chauvinist. He'd trained her himself and he'd led her to believe—

She shook away the thought. And she tried to ignore

the little voice that taunted her, reminding her that Zach had outsold her last year.

Not by much, but he'd won.

He'd won and she'd lost.

Kenneth looked from Maddie to Zach and back to Maddie. "Your future is in your own hands," Kenneth said. "You can win the position, but you have to earn it. I'm speaking to both of you."

A sound like white noise buzzed in Maddie's ears.

"I'm a self-made man," Kenneth continued. "I never had anything handed to me. I built this business from the ground up and I want to make sure my successor not only fosters it, but takes it to places I never dreamed possible."

He punctuated the statement with a shrug.

Self-made man? Never had anything handed to him? Was he kidding?

It took every ounce of Maddie's self-control to keep from reminding him that the Texas Lottery money he'd won hadn't exactly come from hard work and determination. He'd beaten the odds and was lucky enough to choose the right numbers. But she also knew what his retort would be. That he'd invested that money. He hadn't squandered it on all the trappings that a man who'd been raised by a single mother who could barely make ends meet might've been tempted to buy: the fancy house, the expensive cars. She'd heard him tell the story a million times. At face value, a cool million seemed like a lot of money, but it wasn't. In fact, it was just enough to provide a false sense of wealth. After a person lived like a rich man for a few years, all he'd have

left to show for it would be an empty bank account—
and very often he'd be in worse financial shape than
when he'd started.

It was a point of pride for Kenneth that he had been
smart and invested his money. He'd worked hard to
build Fortunado Real Estate into what it was today.

*Yeah, Dad, what about how hard I've worked for
you? What about how much of myself I've invested in
you and Fortunado?*

He glanced at his watch. "I need to leave in a few
moments. I have a lunch appointment and I don't want
to be late. But do you have any questions I can answer
before we adjourn?"

Yeah, Dad, I do. What the hell?

"What are you looking for?" Zach asked. "What's
the criteria?"

Maddie turned and looked at Zach for the first time
since her dad had made the announcement.

Ah! Amateur question, McCarter.

She knew instantly what her father would say before he said it.

Kenneth shrugged. "Show me what you've got.
That's all I'm going to say. Well, that and may the best
man—or woman—win."

Her father held up a finger, his eyes flashing. "Wait.
There is something. You know the Paisley? That new
high-rise Dave Madison is building downtown? I want
Fortunado to be the exclusive agents for that property. I
want you two to work together to land that listing. The
whole building. You need to work together to come up

with a plan to seal the deal. That's an important part of the challenge."

"We're on it." Zach got to his feet, making all the right noises of agreement and understanding. As he shook Kenneth's hand, Maddie stayed in her seat. Zach lingered on the threshold of her father's office, obviously watching to see what she was going to say or do.

Maddie got a little bit of satisfaction from the look on his face when she said, "I need to talk to my father for a moment, Zach. Please excuse us."

"No problem." Zach gave a quick wave of his hand and closed Kenneth's office door behind him.

"How could you do this to me?" She turned to her dad the second they were alone. "I'm your daughter."

She couldn't remember playing this card before. It had been a point of pride to never take advantage of the fact that she was the boss's daughter. She knew she enjoyed a certain level of job security that those without the benefit of Fortunado blood didn't have. But she'd never needed it. She'd worked damn hard to earn the presidency that her father had so unceremoniously announced was up for grabs.

If that's the way he was going to be, then for a few moments she was going to play the family card. She was going to be the boss's daughter because he owed her an explanation—if for nothing else, as to why he'd blindsided her.

She could tell by the look on his face that he could see the depth of her anger.

"I'm sorry, Maddie," he said. "I can understand that this comes as a surprise, but I think you'll appreciate the challenge and rise to the occasion once you have some time to think it through."

She let his words reverberate in the air and took some satisfaction that at least he understood that she was upset.

"I love you," he continued. "I love all my children, but I also don't intend to let you or your siblings get complacent—especially when it comes to the business I've spent my life building. All promotions at Fortunado Real Estate must be earned. I have complete faith that you'll earn yours."

People might have argued that Zach McCarter was a lot of things. One thing they couldn't call him was a quitter. Overly sentimental probably wouldn't be on the list either.

So, why was it, he wondered, as he waited for Maddie at the Blue Moon Cafe, that he couldn't stop thinking about the look on her face when Kenneth had presented the challenge?

This should've been a day to celebrate his shot at the opportunity of a lifetime. This was the payoff for his hard work. Instead, he felt vaguely unsettled thinking about that injured-doe look in Maddie's blue eyes.

She'd probably kick him if she knew he was comparing her to an injured animal. She'd probably buck right up in his face.

But that's what he'd seen and he couldn't get her face out of his head.

This was business. Any other time—any other

person—and Zach wouldn't have given it a second thought. But he had a soft spot for Maddie.

Zach was probably more surprised than Maddie when Kenneth asked them to compete for the position. After all, everyone who worked for Fortunado Real Estate knew that Maddie coveted her father's job. She was the heir apparent, and everyone thought it was a given that she would take over for Kenneth when he retired.

When Kenneth asked him to transfer from San Antonio to the Houston office, Zach knew change was in the air. At first, he thought it was a token gesture to pacify Zach's restlessness. Kenneth seemed good at reading people. Even though Zach hadn't said it, Kenneth had to know that after five years as a broker with Fortunado, it was time for a change, time to open his own real estate office. After all, he was making Fortunado a hell of a lot of money.

Zach had no ties to San Antonio, no family to consider, no reason to not pack up and move to Houston. The move was an opportunity to learn the Houston market, which would be a useful tool once he did strike out on his own. When Kenneth had asked him to come to Houston, he'd said he wanted his senior associates to focus on teamwork, that there was some new construction in the Houston area and he wanted to put together an "A-Team"—Kenneth's words. He hadn't said who else was on his A-Team, but he'd specifically spelled out that he wanted Zach's help assuring that Fortunado would get exclusive listing contracts. Of course, Zach had been up for the challenge, but that teamwork bit threw him. Generally, he worked alone. He rarely partnered with other agents on listings. It wasn't his MO. Of course, it would take teamwork to run a business like Fortunado.

But this—this chance to head Fortunado—it was an unexpected challenge and he liked it. It would take teamwork and maybe this was a good chance for him to prove to himself that he wanted to manage a team rather than flying solo.

It all made sense—the transfer, the invitation to the barbecue where Kenneth announced his intent to retire, and today's meeting where he'd tapped the two of them as front-runners for his position.

The only thing getting in the way of intense satisfaction and immediate strategizing on how to annihilate the competition was that look on Maddie's face.

That's why he'd wanted the two of them to have lunch and sort this out. Kenneth had been smart when he'd tacked on the Paisley addendum. The last thing he needed was for his two top associates to be at war. Not only did they need to sit down and strategize about the Paisley, but they needed to make sure everything was good between them.

Easy for him to say since he was the interloper.

When Maddie walked into the restaurant, their gazes snared. She didn't smile. Her face looked neutral. Again, she seemed to be daring him to look away first—to walk away from the opportunity first.

He stood and watched her walk toward him.

He had two choices: he could bow out or he could go for it. If he chose to go for it, there would be no option but to pull out all the stops, to step up his game. If he stepped up his game, he would win. He always won. It was a point of pride.

Even if this opportunity didn't feel 100 percent right and it felt as if he was preparing to take something that didn't belong to him, Zach McCarter had never been a quitter.

He needed to put his game face on now. That face didn't have to be mean or savage. The mark of a good manager was to deal with conflict and produce as many win-wins as possible—especially in situations like this where there could only be one winner.

Him.

He would need Maddie on his team when that happened.

"Zach," she said, as she reached the table.

"Maddie, thanks for agreeing to meet on such short notice."

He reached for her chair, but she pulled it out herself. "Of course," she said. "There's a lot at stake here."

He nodded.

"That's why it's even more important that we work together," she said.

He wasn't sure what he'd expected, but based on the way she'd received the news not even two hours earlier, her eagerness to work together came as a shock. The woman was full of surprises.

"I'm glad you feel that way," he said. "We're going to make a great team."

Chapter Three

"Ping-Pong is not a date," Maddie said to Schuyler as she drove her sister and Carlo to see a house in the Austin neighborhood of Westlake. She'd driven up to Austin to show them houses and commercial property for a nightclub Carlo wanted to open. Carlo had been looking for months and holding out for exactly the right spot to open his new business. He'd come close a couple of times with property Maddie had shown him. Now that he was getting married, Maddie had a feeling he'd settle down and make a decision on the commercial site.

This trip was a welcome opportunity to get away from the office—to put some space between Zach and herself. If only Schuyler would stop making Zach tag along in spirit. "Or at least it's not the kind of first date I'm interested in."

Liar. If circumstances were different, you'd be happy to pick up trash with Zach McCarter and call it a fun first date.

But the situation was what it was. And it wasn't fun.

"Besides," Maddie added, "I cannot believe you'd even mention Zach McCarter in that context now that Dad has pitted us against each other."

After the disastrous meeting with her father and subsequent tension-charged lunch with Zach, she'd driven home, thrown the basics into an overnight tote and driven the two and a half hours to Austin. Presumably, it was to show Schuyler and Carlo property. But, if she was perfectly honest with herself, it had been for self-preservation.

She'd never been so happy to get out of the office—to get out of town. Because suddenly the entire city of Houston seemed too small to accommodate the dreams and ambitions of both Zach and her.

It was clear one of them had to go.

And it wouldn't be her.

Just because she was working out of town, it didn't mean she would be the one to bow out. They had their marching orders. They would work together to secure the Paisley deal and sell out the luxury high-rise. In fact, she'd taken the initiative to call Dave Madison's assistant and set up a meeting. He was out of town and Monday was his first available. In the meantime, she would help her sister and future brother-in-law. Working outside of the office would give her time to clear her head. It would only make her stronger.

"It's totally a date," her sister said. "He is so gorgeous, Mads. Maybe Dad has a method to his madness. Maybe he's doing this to throw you and Zach together? Remember how at the barbecue he said he thought of him as a son? Maybe he meant son-in-law."

Maddie shook her head. "I don't think so. And Sky, I really don't want to talk about him. Okay?"

Now she was sorry she'd told Schuyler about her father's plan. Even so, Schuyler was still going on about Ping-Pong as a first date.

Maddie white-knuckled the steering wheel. Even her siblings supported Maddie as their father's heir apparent. Her three brothers had chosen careers outside of the real estate industry. Valene was just starting out at Fortunado Real Estate. Schuyler had never shown an interest in the family business. Even though she could've had a role at Fortunado, she'd chosen to follow her own path. She'd confessed that there was a time when she'd felt like the odd sibling out—since both of her sisters had been bitten by the real estate bug—but following her own path had brought Schuyler to the Mendoza Winery, and that's where she'd met her husband-to-be. Now, Schuyler seemed to have made peace with her path in life.

And Maddie's once sure life was upside down.

Beside her, Schuyler sighed. "But you guys would look so cute together."

"We would not look cute together." Maddie's voice was monotone.

We would look gorgeous together.

Mortified that Schuyler was going on and on about this in front of Carlo, Maddie glanced in the rearview mirror. She was relieved to see that he'd put his earbuds in and was gazing out the passenger window. He seemed to be nodding his head along to the music and not paying one bit of attention to their conversation.

Thank goodness.

This was sister-talk that they should be discussing in private.

"And just to clarify," Schuyler said, "Ping-Pong would be a sweet first date. You need to lighten up, missy."

Schuyler's personality was like a Chinese finger trap. Once she latched onto something, she grabbed even tighter if the other person tried to pull away. The trick was to relax, to lean into it.

Or make her think she'd hurt your feelings.

"Zach didn't mean anything by it. He's probably forgotten all about it, anyway. So, just drop it, okay? Besides, how could I ever date a guy who was after my job? Please don't make me feel any worse than I already do."

Schuyler's face softened. Then she muttered something under her breath that sounded frighteningly like, *There's no wonder Dad passed you over for the promotion.*

"What did you just say?" Maddie demanded. "That was really mean."

Schuyler flinched. "I said, there's no way Zach would pass on that after we caused such a commotion. What was mean about that?"

Maddie stole a look at her sister. Schuyler looked thoroughly stricken.

"I'm sorry," Maddie conceded. "I must've misunderstood."

They rode in silence for a few moments, until Schuyler bounced back.

"We really did cause a commotion over you two matching up at the Ping-Pong table." Schuyler shifted in her seat so that she was facing Maddie, and continued as if she hadn't heard a word Maddie had said. "Mads, you two would be so perfect. If you start dating now, you can bring him to the wedding. You'll look so good in pictures. Like Barbie and Ken."

Maddie rolled her eyes. "I'm about as far from Barbie as a Tonka truck."

"Stop being so hard on yourself," Schuyler said. "He's totally into you. I can feel it. And with a little…" Schuyler reached out and gently toyed with a lock of Maddie's long blond hair. "With just a little spiffing up, you could totally put Barbie to shame. Barbie ain't got nothin' on you, sister."

Maddie made the mistake of glancing at Schuyler and saw her make a gesture that was a combination of double finger guns, a shrug and pursed lips.

"What?" Schuyler laughed. "Don't look at me that way. It's true. But don't be insulted. That wasn't a dig at your looks. You're gorgeous, Mads. But you could be like Hollywood-level *gorge* if you just made a few changes."

Okay. Here we go.

Maddie felt her walls going up. Schuyler was the pretty sister. Maddie had always been the smart sister. Not the smartest *sibling*—her brothers had that sewed up. Valene was the baby, so, somehow, she escaped being compared to any of them.

Lucky Val.

Too bad society often valued looks over substance. Not that Sky lacked substance. She just… Well, sometimes Schuyler got away with things because she was pretty. She smiled and batted her big blue eyes and men turned to putty in her hands.

Sky wasn't manipulative. Not exactly. She didn't have a mean bone in her body. What she did have was this almost childlike, free-spirited quality and a general lack of self-consciousness that allowed her to get away with things that Maddie would never even dream of trying.

Maddie didn't have time to worry about the latest fashions and lipsticks. Classic wardrobe pieces and a no-nonsense grooming routine had always served her well. She wore her long, thick blond hair one length so she could let it dry naturally and pull it back from her face, which was always makeup-free, except for a swipe of clear lip gloss on special occasions. She had been blessed with good skin. So, why take a chance of clogging her pores with makeup she didn't have time to mess with anyway?

"Comparing a woman to Barbie isn't exactly a compliment, Sky. And last I heard, Ken wasn't interested in Barbie. I don't think she's his type, if you know what I mean. Not that there's anything wrong with Ken's preference. You know, love is love is love. I believe in live and let love, whatever floats his boat. Right now, my preference is to focus on work."

Yeah, and look where that had gotten her. A first-class ticket to nowhere. For a split second her life flashed before her eyes and she didn't like what she saw: still single; the spinster sister. Her nieces and nephews would call her Crazy Old Aunt Maddie. Only, instead of cats, she'd have a whole herd of corgis.

When she glanced at Schuyler, her sister was frowning.

"If you ask me," Schuyler said, "I think you're protesting too much, sister dear."

Maddie felt heat bloom at her chest and begin to work its way up.

Maybe, she *was* protesting too much. She was giving herself away. So, she seized the opportunity to grab the layup her sister had presented like a gift.

"I don't remember asking you, Sky. In fact, I have no idea what you're talking about. What am I overprotesting?"

"All I'm saying is you'd have to be dead not to notice how drop-dead gorgeous Zach McCarter is. Or oblivious. Maybe my sister is oblivious." Schuyler directed the comment to Carlo in the back seat, as if Maddie wasn't even there. "A hot guy is interested in her and she's oblivious."

Carlo didn't answer.

Maddie stole another glance in the rearview mirror and was relieved to see that Carlo's earbuds were still in place. He was the one who seemed to be oblivious. Thank God.

"Don't talk about me like I'm not here," Maddie protested. "And don't pull Carlo into this. FYI, when I'm

in the office, I focus on my job, I don't ogle my co-
workers."

"Are you really so focused on your work that you
can't see what's right in front of you?"

Even though Maddie's eyes were glued to the road,
she felt her sister's gaze boring into her as the heat that
had been confined to her chest crept up her neck until
it burned her cheeks.

Schuyler clapped her hands. "Oh, my God. You *do*
see him. You like him, don't you?"

For a fraction of a second Maddie felt all her defenses
give way and every schoolgirl emotion wash over her
face. And even though Schuyler could only see her in
profile she obviously saw it, too.

"You are totally into him!" she said. "Carlo, she likes
him."

All Maddie could do was shake her head like an
idiot.

"Mads, it's okay. There's nothing wrong with having a crush on a guy. I mean, especially at your age."

Maddie slanted a look of death at her sister.

"Thanks for that, Sky. You always know how to
make me feel good."

"I didn't mean to upset you," Schuyler said. "You
know what I mean."

Yes, she did. And her sister was right. She was
twenty-nine years old and single with no romantic prospects. It shouldn't matter. It didn't matter because she
was married to her job. Yet, she couldn't even admit
that she had a crush on Zach McCarter. And why not?
Carlo wasn't listening and Schuyler was a safe confi-

dant. For all her free-spirited ways, she'd also proven herself to be trustworthy—a virtual vault…after she wore you down and made you confess.

For a moment, Maddie let herself wonder if the co-worker excuse was simply another part of her defense mechanism.

It was. She had enough self-awareness to admit that. But it was also true that if she admitted her attraction to Zach and things got weird, she might lose one of the firm's best brokers.

There she was overthinking it again—

But that's why she was good at her job. She thought things through. Where Schuyler would leap and hope the net appeared, Maddie looked at pros and cons from every angle before taking one step.

The overriding fact was, she and Zach had worked together for five years. Albeit, they'd been in different offices. They'd had five years to flirt. They'd had five years to act on any possible feelings or chemistry or electricity—whatever you wanted to label it. If he'd been interested, if he'd had any feelings for her, he would've acted on them by now. He hadn't. Clearly, he wasn't interested.

Even though she'd crushed on him from afar, that ship had sailed. Her father had pitted them against each other and she was going to win the promotion. So, it would be an exercise in frustration to try and start up something now. Even if it wouldn't be wildly inappropriate for the brand-new president to date one of her employees, she wouldn't have any time for a

new relationship—or even a date. She would have her
hands full with work.

Maddie knew the only way to get Schuyler off her
back was to give a little, but lay down the law.

"Of course Zach is gorgeous. Everybody knows Zach
is gorgeous. Zach knows Zach is gorgeous. He's simply not my type."

"I don't know, Mads," Schuyler said. "I felt some
serious chemistry zinging back and forth between the
two of you."

Enough!

For a moment, Maddie was tempted to lash out, to
tell her sister that she had much more important things
to worry about than handsome faces and zinging chemistry. But she caught herself before she did. She bit her
lip a little too hard to make her unkind words dissipate.
And good thing. It was her fatal flaw—when she got
defensive, when she felt like she'd been backed into a
corner, she tended to come out swinging. Being mean
to Schuyler would be like kicking a puppy, which she
would never do. Her sister didn't have a mean bone in
her entire body. If Maddie knew what was good for her
she would try to be a little more like her impractical,
impetuous little sister.

Really, she knew it was futile to wish she could be
more like Schuyler, who lived for the moment and put
her heart's desire above all that was practical—hence,
her determination to go against their father's wishes
and follow a lead she believed would prove that their
family, with its Fortunado last name, was related to the
infamous Fortune family.

Maddie steered the car off the high road and onto the street of the Westlake neighborhood home she was sure was perfect for Schuyler and Carlo. And not a moment too soon.

"We're here," Maddie announced as she flicked on her right signal and turned onto the brick driveway of a house that looked like a smaller reproduction of a Spanish castle.

She knew her sister well enough to know she was easily distracted by shiny objects. Right on cue, Schuyler's eyes widened and her jaw dropped. "This is it? Oh, Maddie, it's beautiful. It's just perfect. Carlo, look!"

Carlo had pulled out the earbuds and was echoing his fiancée's awe.

There was nothing like a piece of gorgeous real estate to reframe a conversation. Perched high atop a hill, overlooking Lake Austin, this house was a particularly stunning show-stealer. Carlo and his cousins had recently opened Mendoza Winery in the Hill Country and business was booming. Though this estate was at the upper end of the couple's price range, the bank had prequalified them for it.

"This is it," Maddie said, as she took off her seat belt. "First and foremost, the backyard is fenced in for the dogs." Schuyler had recently rescued two little dogs named Stuff and Fluff. "It features four bedrooms, three baths, a gourmet kitchen, with a keeping room, a media center, exercise and sauna, wine cellar and tasting room, pool and spa, a guest apartment, and a three-car garage. Would you like to see inside?"

"What's a keeping room?" Carlo asked.

"It's an open-plan room that flows right off the kitchen," Maddie said.

She let herself out of the car and joined her sister and Carlo, who were staring up at the house like they'd found the Holy Grail.

"Could you see yourselves here?" Maddie asked.

Schuyler nodded. "This is our house, Carlo."

Carlo laughed. "It's impressive, but we haven't even seen the inside yet."

"I know," Schuyler said. "But I just know this is our house."

"Well, come on in and have a look around." Maddie took the lead and started toward the oversize dark wooden double doors.

This was why she loved her job. She was good at it. Matching couples and families with their dream homes was like a sixth sense for her. When she was doing that, and getting a reaction like she'd gotten from Schuyler and Carlo, she was in her glory. Setting up people with houses was so much more comfortable than allowing herself to be matched for a relationship—or pitted against the only man she could've seen herself getting involved with.

It was all for the best. She hadn't always made the best decisions where men were concerned. A lot of time had passed since her last mistake. Nonetheless, it was a lesson learned. That's why even if the electricity between Zach and her burned bright the way Schuyler claimed it did, Maddie had to pull the plug.

* * *

The GPS indicated that Zach's destination was approaching on the left. He turned down the Tim McGraw song that was playing on the radio, flicked on his signal and slowed down before he steered the behemoth of a pickup truck he'd rented for the occasion onto the apron of the driveway, stopping in front of an impressive black iron gate. He pushed the button on the call box. After Zach identified himself, the person connected to the voice on the other end buzzed him in.

As he followed the long, winding gravel road past stands of pine trees and fenced-in pastureland, he took the opportunity to survey what he could see of the property—and it was vast.

With more than three thousand acres of unspoiled Hill Country farmland, the Pomodoro Ranch in Sisterdale was a gem. He already sensed it had been worth the nearly four-hour drive from Houston. Or at least it would be once he secured the listing. He silently vowed that he was not leaving here until he had a signed agreement.

That's why he'd pulled out all the stops and had changed into boots, jeans and a chambray work shirt, which he'd washed three times to take away the just-purchased look of it. The ensemble was far from his usual style, but he figured Jim and Mary Ann Winters, owners of the Pomodoro, would be more comfortable with someone dressed in Texas casual than a guy who arrived in a convertible BMW and looked like he was ready to grab a nine iron and hit the golf course.

He'd also made sure his ride was as much of an accessory as the Stetson sitting on the seat next to him. The Ford F-150 wasn't his Beemer by any stretch of the imagination, but it had proven to be a surprisingly comfortable ride.

The gravel road delivered him in front of a rambling wooden and brick colonial ranch-style house with an awe-inducing six-car garage and double beveled-glass front doors. Zach parked in the generous area in front of the house that was finished in pavers.

Before he'd closed the door to the truck's cab, a man in a cowboy hat, faded, work-worn jeans and a plaid shirt, who looked to be upwards of seventy, had stepped outside and was offering his hand.

"You Zach McCarter?" he drawled.

"Yes, sir. That would be me." He met the man's hand with a firm shake. "Mr. Winters, nice to meet you."

"Thanks for making the drive all the way out here, son," Jim Winters said. "The location scares off some people from the city. I guess you could say that's the first test I've been putting Realtors through since I started interviewing brokers. But I heard you were the very best. Is that the truth?"

"I'll do everything in my power to make sure you're not disappointed."

He wished he could say he was the best, but a certain competitive blue-eyed blonde had been giving him a run for that honor. Lately, the visceral reaction he felt when he thought of her made him realize that if circumstances were different—if he didn't work for her father, if they weren't competing for the same job that would make one of them the boss and leave the other gravely disappointed—he might want to see what else the two of them could excel at together. And it wouldn't be anything that could happen at the office.

But he couldn't think about Maddie right now. For the last few days, since their meeting with Kenneth, Zach had been telling himself to keep his mind in the game and his efforts focused on proving that he was the man for the job. And that started with landing this listing.

"You up for walking the land?" Jim Winters asked.

"I can't think of anything I'd rather do right now."

The older man nodded. "This ranch has been in my family for three generations. But my boys moved out years ago, and they have their own families and lives. Seems like no one is interested in ranching these days. That's why Mary Ann and I decided the best thing we could do is sell the place. Do you think you can find me a buyer, son?"

Several hours later, Zach parked in an open space near the front doors of the high-rise building that housed the Fortunado office. He'd just gotten back to town after the listing appointment in Sisterdale. It was after business hours—if the real estate industry had *business hours*. All the top producers worked way beyond the usual Monday-through-Friday, nine-to-five gig. It was Friday night and he had about an hour's work left before he could call it a day. It didn't feel like a sacrifice to Zach. In fact, he felt more at home at the office than he did at his condo.

First, he wanted to change out of the Wranglers and

chambray work shirt he'd worn to the appointment with Jim and Mary Ann Winters. His regular outfit of khakis and a button-down was neatly hanging on hangers on a hook behind his office door. The way he looked at it, he wasn't being disingenuous by wearing the Wranglers and Stetson, as much as he was giving the clients what they wanted. And it had worked. He'd landed the listing. His tenth listing this week.

As he unlocked the front door and secured it behind him, he noticed a light was on in the office across the hall from his. Maddie's office.

It shouldn't be a surprise. The only other person who rivaled him for hours worked was Maddie. He hadn't seen her car in the parking lot, and thought she might have called it an early day.

Obviously, he'd miscalculated.

She was fierce, competitive and hungry—eager to take down her competition and slow to back down. Those were the perks that came from growing up wealthy and entitled. She possessed a confidence he'd never been afforded growing up in the foster care system. His father had worked himself to death—literally— leaving his mother to raise Zach and his brother on her own. She died two years later, when Zach was fifteen and his brother Rich was twenty-one. Technically, Rich had been old enough to be Zach's guardian, but he said he wasn't up for the responsibility. For lack of knowing better and trusting that her oldest son would do right by his younger brother, their mother had named Rich the beneficiary of the life insurance policy she'd had through her job. It had gone a long way toward putting Rich through law school. The deal was supposed to be once Rich graduated and got established, he would put Zach through college. But in order to get through law school, he'd said he needed to be free to pull all-nighters at the library without the responsibility of a moody, grieving teenage brother who skipped school and got into trouble.

His grandparents were dead and his one aunt and uncle had been estranged from his mother, so Zach had nowhere to go. Whether it was at the behest of the authorities or because Rich didn't know how—or want—to fight for him, Zach ended up in foster care. He bounced around the system. He'd hidden how scared and abandoned he'd felt behind a facade of independence and toughness. The big takeaway from that three-year period of his life was that it was best not to depend on anyone.

But in the end, Zach liked to believe the experience hadn't made him bitter. In fact, he liked to think it had turned him into the man he'd become. He'd learned to not get too close to anyone and only rely on himself. That way, he knew he'd never be let down. Self-reliance had been the only sure thing in his life.

Once that had become ingrained, he'd learned that a smile and a lighthearted demeanor could open doors and give him access to people who could help him pad his bank account. Case in point: who would've ever thought that Kenneth Fortunado would open the door to his empire to somebody who didn't share his blood?

Zach had earned his way to this offer. He hadn't strong-armed or swindled or misled Fortunado into making this offer. He'd simply shown him that he was the best person for the job.

That's why it was even more important to not let the stricken expression on Maddie's face distract him from his goal. Kenneth had said, *May the best man— or woman—win.* Zach refused to feel guilty for trying.

He made his way down the dimly lit hall and paused in the threshold of her office door.

"Did someone forget to tell you you could go home?" he joked.

"What are you talking about?" Maddie said, without missing a beat. "This is home. I thought you'd cut out early—what the hell are you wearing?"

She scrunched up her nose and gave him a once-over from head to toe, then added, "What costume party are you attending?"

"I had an appointment," Zach said.

"Where? Billy Bob's Rodeo Clown School? This is a new look for you. And maybe not quite your style."

He smirked. At least she was still acting like herself. He shouldn't be surprised, he told himself. She was a professional. The Madeleine Fortunado he knew would never let anyone catch her brooding in the office.

"That's one of the reasons I came back to the office," he told her. "To change clothes."

Maddie grimaced. "You really went to your appointment dressed like that?"

"Sure. I bought the hat especially for the occasion." He tipped it onto his head. "Too bad you didn't get to see the truck. It pulled everything together."

She'd been in Austin on business for a few days and

he'd been out of the office closing some deals. They hadn't seen each other since their lunch on Monday.

He was glad to see her acting like herself.

"The truck?" she asked. "What are you talking about?"

She rolled her chair back from her desk and crossed one shapely, tanned leg over the other. The move inched her gray skirt up her leg a bit. Zach dared himself not to let his gaze fall.

"The ranch is over in Sisterdale. I rented a Ford F-150 to complete the ensemble." He gestured to his too-blue Wranglers. "I figured I might as well look the part when I met the client."

Maddie smirked as she smoothed her skirt down. "You know, ranchers can usually smell an imposter a mile away."

He cocked a brow. "Are you suggesting I'm not genuine?"

Maddie gave his ensemble a very slow, obvious head-to-toe perusal. He didn't mind her eyes on him one bit.

With the sleeves pushed up on his forearms, he looked unnervingly natural in that blue work shirt that emphasized his broad shoulders and trim waist where it was tucked into jeans. Damn if those Wranglers didn't fit him like he'd been wearing them for years. He'd finished the ensemble with cowboy boots that somehow were just scuffed enough to look authentic.

This was proof that the guy could wear anything and look hot.

"Given the fact that you drive a sports car and probably spend more money on a single suit than I spend on clothes for the entire year, yes, I'd say this is not a *genuine* look for you."

But damn, you look good—

Maddie bit back the words before they could escape and made a noise that was somewhere between a cough and clearing her throat as she made sure she swallowed them.

"Are you okay?" Zach asked.

Maddie waved him off. "Of course. I just have a tickle in my throat. Please tell me you didn't actually wear the cowboy hat."

"I did wear the cowboy hat. Why? Do you think I shouldn't have?"

That delicious mouth of his had turned up at the corners and Maddie knew he was trying to yank her chain. She was determined to play along, just as she was determined to prove to him that she wasn't the least bit affected by her father's bombshell, that she was secure in the challenge and would succeed easily in claiming what was rightfully hers.

But why Zach? Why did her dad have to challenge her with Zach? If he wanted to prove a point, he could've brought in someone from the outside. He could've poached a competitor or recruited some hotshot who raked in millions of dollars in sales.

No, he'd chosen Zach. Her crush. He didn't know that, of course.

"Maddie?" Zach said. "The hat? Shouldn't I have worn the hat?"

"Only if you wanted to look like an even bigger fool."

He winced. "Next time I'll know better."

"I suppose you bought the belt buckle, too?" Her gaze dropped to the oversize, square silver belt buckle that featured a gold-toned steer head right in the center.

"Yeah." His gaze dropped, too. She knew that he knew that her gaze had fallen due south. She crossed her arms to keep him from seeing the shudder of longing that rippled through her.

"It's a beauty, isn't it?"

Maddie swallowed hard and forced her eyes up.

"So, when are they going to make their decision?" she asked.

He smiled at her and she could've sworn he seemed happy that she'd been looking at him. God, she loved the way his blue eyes crinkled at the corners when he smiled. Eyes like that could sink ships and break hearts.

Right this moment was proof positive of that.

She needed to be careful. He was the enemy. The one person standing between her and everything she'd been working for. Yet, she couldn't resist flirting with him. Hell, forget the flirting. She wanted to walk right up to him and unbutton that blue shirt and see if his abs were as washboard flat as they looked. She wanted to relieve him of that belt with the ridiculous buckle and slip her hands beneath the waistband of those Wranglers and see if his hidden assets looked as promising as advertised.

"What do you mean?" he said.

She bit her bottom lip. "I mean are they talking to other brokers? When are they going to let you know?"

"Of course, they're not talking to other brokers. Do

you think I went to all this trouble and drove all the way out to Sisterdale to walk away without the listing?"

"You got the listing? Dressed like that?"

"Of course I did."

Maddie felt her cheeks flame as a little voice inside her said, *This is why your father is giving him a shot.* The logical part of her knew this was true, even though the emotional part of her swelled up and eclipsed the voice of reason.

She wasn't about to let him know it bothered her.

"Good for you," she said. "I guess it was worth dressing like a greenhorn."

He could have made a comment about going the extra mile and how it might do her some good to get out of her comfort zone and think outside the box like he did.

But he didn't.

All he said was, "Looks that way. Listen, I need to go finish up the paperwork."

"Right," Maddie said. "Are you going to the Thirsty Ox for happy hour?"

On Friday nights, a handful of Houston-area real estate professionals had a standing date to meet for drinks and compare notes. They were supposed to share tips and tricks, but mostly, it was a report card for the week, a show-and-tell as to who'd sold what and had secured the most listings. It was a license to brag and posture, masquerading as cooperative business. He hadn't been part of anything like that in San Antonio.

"That's right." Zach glanced at his watch. "That is tonight. I have to finish my paperwork, and I have a thing later tonight, but I think I can stop by for a few minutes."

It wasn't that he disliked sharing; he just wasn't used to operating that way. This was business. He didn't see how it helped to brag about your clients and closings. But to each his own. In the name of self-correction, he knew being more community-minded could only help him in his effort to win the Fortunado promotion. Kenneth was a social guy. In most regards, it was the only area in which he and Fortunado differed. Zach had always held his business ventures close to the chest, Kenneth's philosophy was that glad-handing only bolstered his business.

Maddie cocked a brow at him. "You have a *thing*? Is that a technical term or a formal occasion?"

He laughed. "Neither. It's just a *thing*. Don't you ever have *things*?"

"Can't say I do," she said. "I'm usually too busy working for that kind of nonsense."

"You need to get out more, Madeleine," he said.

Maddie was pretty in a natural way that some men might overlook, though her natural beauty wasn't lost on him. She had smooth skin, which she didn't hide with makeup. Her clothing usually leaned toward the expensively understated. While her clothes were never flashy or, God forbid, sexy, Zach recognized the good quality of the classics she chose. She usually wore her long blond hair pulled back off her face with a headband or ponytail. Tonight, she'd twisted it on top of her head and secured it with a yellow pencil. He considered ribbing her about her improvised hairstyle in the same fashion in which she'd kidded him about his faux cowboy ensemble, but he thought better of it. Not tonight. Not when he still had work to do and then he had to go out to real estate show-and-tell.

As he stood there, he realized he wasn't sure how much they should tell the happy hour gang about the way Kenneth was auditioning his replacement.

Maddie was a strong woman. In fact, some considered her downright prickly, which probably added to her untouchable quality. It was something that transcended the unspoken off-limits mandate of her being the boss's daughter. With her Ivy League education and her sheltered upbringing, a woman like Maddie was way out of his league. Besides, in the little bit of time he had for pleasure, he wasn't looking for anything too serious or heavy. There would be plenty of time for that, after he'd secured his future. For now, he needed to keep his eye on the prize.

"We need to talk about your father's announcement and how we want to handle it if it comes up tonight," he said. "It has the potential to make things uncomfortable between us, but I want you to know that it doesn't have to be."

"Okay." Her answer was remarkably level and devoid of emotion. He'd hoped that if she had a problem with it or harbored any resentment or lingering animosity toward him—Monday at their lunch it was apparent that she wasn't happy with the arrangement—he hoped they could talk it out.

"If you need to say anything to me, now is the time

to say it," he said. "Go ahead. Don't hold back. I can take it."

She looked at him as if he'd sprouted two heads.

"Such as you won't be offended if I tell you how much you're annoying me right now by talking to me instead of letting me get my work done? Is that what you mean?"

Her blue eyes flashed a mischievous glint as she smiled at him. There wasn't a trace of the hurt and animosity he'd sensed days ago. In fact, he half expected her to good-naturedly accuse him of trying to undermine her, but she didn't. So, he took it as his cue to exit.

He smiled back and held up his hands. "Sorry. I'll leave you to your work."

As he started toward his office, she said, "Zach?"

He turned back to her. "Yes?"

"You know I intend to win. What are you going to do when I do? I mean… Will you stay?"

They both needed to get to work. He wasn't going to stand here and go back and forth about who was going to win. They both wanted it.

"Honestly? I don't see how I could stay if I don't get the promotion. So, that means we're both in it to win it."

"I guess we are," she said. "Bring it on."

Chapter Four

Bring it on?

Maddie cringed inwardly as she replayed the conversation she'd had with Zach an hour ago in the office. She shouldn't have said it—again. It made her sound bitter and spiteful...and uncool. Not that she'd ever been cool a single day in her life.

She should've just kept playing it cool. But once again, she'd tacked on those final three words: *Bring it on*.

If Zach was going to leave Fortunado if—when—she won the promotion, then she might as well kiss him and get it out of her system.

She inhaled sharply at the rogue thought. She blinked and took a gulp of beer, glancing around the Thirsty Ox looking for colleagues, as if they might be able to read her mind if they were close by. The thought was ridiculous. Both thoughts were ridiculous: mind-reading colleagues and kissing Zach to get him out of her system.

But was it such a bad idea?

She was going to win. He was going to leave—and who could blame him? If Zach bested her for the promotion, would she really want to stay around? It wasn't that either of them were sore losers. It was a matter of principle, of self-preservation.

If he was going to leave anyway, why not just kiss him now and get it out of her system? Then she would be able to clear her mind—cleanse it of all lustful Zach McCarter thoughts—and better focus on the colossal task ahead of her. Because once she kissed Zach, it would be like popping a balloon. The illusion would be debunked. The great and powerful Oz would be exposed to be a mere mortal.

If that were true, then why were her lips tingling at the thought of tasting his, and her girl parts bucking for more than a kiss?

Oh, hell.

She crossed her legs, trying to stanch the need. Even though she thought she might want more, she told herself one taste would be enough to send her feelings for him into a downward spiral. That's how it had always worked in the past. A big buildup, only for the fireworks to fizzle out with a pitiful whimper.

Kissing Zach would be no exception.

Where is everyone?

Now, more than ever, she needed the distraction of colleagues talking shop. She'd arrived at the Thirsty

Ox a little later than usual since she'd been late getting out of the office. Usually, she was the first one here on Friday nights, single-handedly holding down the fort until the rest of their group arrived. But as she was wrapping up her day at the office, she'd figured someone else could man up and hold the tables—usually the three six-toppers in the center of the pub. But when she'd walked in, she was surprised to discover she was, as always, the first to arrive.

The Thirsty Ox was their place of choice. There was an English pub in the front, where people could meet and order drinks and pub fare. In the back was a full-service restaurant. The casual atmosphere and delicious food made it a popular place, and it was busy every day of the week, but at Friday happy hour, it was a madhouse.

By this time, they were all usually on their second or third beers, the ones who'd decided to stay later were considering adjourning to the restaurant in the back where they could enjoy offerings such as fish and chips and shepherd's pie. The ones who were just doing a drive-by were contemplating their departure.

Where was everyone?

She glanced around the place, its Tudor décor embellished with neon beer signs and perennial Christmas tree lights. The pub buzzed with groups playing darts and shooting pool amid the noisy music. But Maddie recognized no one—or had somehow missed them. It was a casual arrangement. No one RSVP'd, and not everyone could make it every week, but there had never been an instance in the five or so years that they'd been meeting that everyone had been absent on the same night.

Everyone except for her. Because this was her big night out every week.

A little voice deep inside hollered up from the darkness, *You're twenty-nine years old. What if you've put all your eggs in one basket for nothing? If Zach wins, what will you do?*

Zach wasn't going to win. Kissing him would be her lucky charm, the motivator that would drive her over the finish line.

But what was she going to do? Walk up and plant a big smacker on him?

That's romantic.

There's nothing romantic about this.

Her lady parts begged to differ. *There could be.*

She got up from the bar and glanced in the back to see if her colleagues had skipped happy hour and headed straight to dinner. When she didn't see anyone, she grabbed a table for four that was newly open. Maybe others were late, or maybe they had other plans. Her sister Val had a date tonight. Maybe everyone had dates tonight. Zach had mentioned that he had plans. Maybe after the unceremonious brush-off she'd given him, he'd decided to skip happy hour and go straight to his thing that he had this evening.

Maybe she was the only one who didn't have a personal life outside of the office.

Maddie took another pull from the long-neck beer bottle, which she'd purchased just as happy hour was winding down. If no one showed by the time she finished her drink, she'd call it a night.

Why was she taking this so personally? The Friday night meet-up wasn't mandatory. It wasn't as if the lot of them had blown off her personal party. But she always looked forward to these get-togethers. It was the one time during the week that she let down her hair and blew off steam.

She really did need to get a life, didn't she?

Work had been her life. It was her boyfriend, her lover. She'd been so focused on climbing the corporate ladder, she hadn't had time to meet men and date. What a fool she'd been.

Her mind kept replaying her father telling her that there was no guarantee, that just because she was his daughter, he wasn't going to hand her the job.

All promotions must be earned.

When had she given him the impression that she was just sitting there waiting for him to hand it to her? That was the humiliating and maddening part. Maddie thought she was showing him her best by putting in eighteen-hour days, working weekends and forgoing vacations and dating. Obviously, her best wasn't good enough.

It'd been good enough to earn her the title of vice president of sales. Zach hadn't earned that title. He was just an associate broker who had a higher level of certification and experience than a basic real estate agent. Granted, he worked hard, but she was *family*. Even if her father thought they both had worked hard and saw the need for a tiebreaker, wouldn't blood win out in the end? How could he potentially pass her over for an outsider?

"Excuse me," said a guy who was part of a large rowdy group a few tables over. "Mind if I take a couple of these chairs?"

"I do mind," Maddie snapped, but tacked on a smile to ease the bluntness of her words. "I'm expecting friends."

Did he really think she came here by herself on a Friday night to have a beer alone at a table for four in the middle of a busy pub? Obviously so.

"Sorry," he murmured. As he turned to walk away, she called him back.

"On second thought," she said. "You can have them. I don't think I'm going to stay much longer."

"What about your friends?" he asked.

Apparently, they're not coming. They'd either been in and out of the place before she'd arrived or she was the only agent with free time on her hands on a Friday night. She could do the solo-girl bit at home, where she was more comfortable and looked less lonely.

"I guess they'll just have to fend for themselves."

The guy's concern lasted about as long as it took his biceps to bulge as he lifted two of the three chairs like he was curling dumbbells. "Cool."

As he walked away with the chairs, someone else came up behind Maddie and put a hand on one of the chairs. Without looking up, she said, "Sorry, someone else is using that chair."

"Who?" asked a familiar voice. "Did you bring a date?"

Her gaze snapped up as Zach sat down in the chair before the guy could return to claim it.

"No, I didn't bring a date," Maddie said. "I gave away the chairs since no one showed up tonight. He's coming back for that one, too."

"He can't have it. I'm using it," he said. "Where is everyone else?"

"Since I'm not the one in charge of this week's RSVPs, your guess is as good as mine."

Zach flinched and she realized she sounded snarky. She didn't mean to. He didn't deserve it.

"Do you want to talk?" he said.

"Talk about what?"

He arched a brow at her in a knowing look and she got the feeling that his patience wasn't infinite. That was fine. She didn't need the charity of his good nature. They were, after all, competitors.

She'd told Zach to *bring it on*.

Ugh.

One of them would win and the other would lose. It was that simple. Anything she divulged—including how unfair, how sexist, how messed up this whole situation felt—would just be tipping her hand. She would be confessing her own self-doubt and that would give him a big advantage.

She wouldn't say anything, but that didn't stop her from feeling every bit of outrage and disappointment. Nor did it stop the endless loop of inner monologue that played in her head.

On top of that, she was mad at herself for letting Zach get under her skin.

Winning should've been enough of an incentive to stay focused, to not let him get to her. But here he was with his sexy eyes and those adorable dimples and he was just making things worse. She should do something to take back her power—something that would give her no choice but to channel all her angry, petulant energy away from those lips and into winning.

"Are you sure there isn't something you want to talk about?" he asked.

As if he didn't know.

"What's there to talk about?"

He laughed. "Okay. I get it. You don't want to talk about it. But just an hour ago in the office, you seemed fine. Now you seem angry."

"I'm not angry. Why would I be angry?" she answered as a server came to take his drink order. The petite twentysomething blonde took on a dreamy quality when Zach smiled at her. Maddie couldn't blame her. Zach had that effect on most women under the age of ninety-five.

"I'll get this round," he said. "What are you drinking?"

"Don't you have a date tonight?" Maddie reminded him.

"A date?" he said as if he didn't understand. "I have plans later, but I don't know if I'd call it a date. What do you want to drink?"

She asked for another beer and Zach ordered the same along with a basket of the restaurant's homemade sweet potato chips.

A Mumford & Sons–type band took the stage and

started playing a loud folksy British-sounding tune. A group of four women stood up and began singing along and clapping with their arms over their heads. Someone in the room let out a long, loud whistle.

Maddie was looking around the room, everywhere but at him.

When the server left, she asked, "Are you meeting a woman?"

"Does it matter?"

"Well, I know I wouldn't appreciate it if a guy showed up for a date with beer breath."

"Good to know. I'll use some mouthwash."

"So, it is a date, then," she said, as if she'd tricked him into the confession.

"So, it does matter to you, then," he answered, a wide grin overtaking his handsome face.

The words were on the tip of her tongue. She tried to bite them back, but she was too late.

"And what if it does?"

In a split second, everything happened in slow motion. Zach's jaw dropped... and she leaned in and kissed him.

It was a whisper of a kiss, so unexpected—even to herself—that she felt his surprise as she braced her hands against his chest. But then, like sweet milk chocolate melting in the heat of the sun, his hard mouth softened and he kissed her back. He took control of the kiss, slowly at first, with lips and hints of tongue, his arms on her back.

His mouth tasted of mint and it fused with the hoppy flavor of the beer she'd been drinking. There was something else, an indefinable flavor that was uniquely him—something which she suddenly realized she'd been craving her entire life. She leaned in closer, not wanting the kiss to end. As if reading her mind, he slid his arms up to her neck, and opened his mouth, deepening the kiss, pulling her closer and sliding his hands into her hair.

The kiss faded into a gradual—almost reluctant— parting of lips, a tentative reclaiming of personal space, a cautious *oh,* Scheisse, *what do we do now?*

In the seconds that followed, she realized that the one kiss that she thought would cure her wasn't working that way at all.

She pressed her fingers to her lips.

As it turned out, kissing Zach to get him out of her system might not have been the cure-all she thought it would be. In fact, it might have opened Pandora's box.

Clearly, she hadn't thought this through as carefully as she'd thought she had; she'd simply reacted, followed her instincts, allowed the pin that held her heart together to be drawn to the steel magnet that was him. If she'd thought it through, common sense would've stopped her from doing something so imprudent. Something so deliciously, divinely, toe-curlingly stupid.

She took a deep breath and reminded herself that now the die was cast. With one kiss, she'd sealed their fate: she had to win and he had to go.

Maddie stood up. "I have to go."

No, he has to go. I have to leave.

"No, you don't," he said. "Because we have some

things we need to talk about. You can't just kiss me and run away."

She grabbed her purse and fled the bar like Cinderella running against midnight.

"Maddie," Zach said. "Don't leave."

But the noisy pub swallowed up his words before they could reach her. Not that it would've done any good if she'd heard him.

With her kiss fresh on his lips, he had to go after her. He stood and pulled a twenty out of his wallet and handed it to the bemused waitress who'd come with their drinks. "Keep the change."

He took a few steps away from the table and scanned the area between him and the door. The place wasn't that big, but he didn't see her.

Madeleine Fortunado was a complicated woman. She was well-bred, but she had a fiery temper. She was fluent in three languages, but she drank American beer from a bottle—in an English pub. She wore very little makeup but she dressed in expensive classics. She had all the quiet tells of a woman who had been raised with every advantage, but she rarely called attention to herself.

Except when she was spontaneously kissing him.

Sure, she was fun to flirt with and, on a very superficial level, he'd thought about dating her, but he'd ruled it out just as fast because she was the boss's daughter. But damn…he'd never wanted her in a physical way. Until now.

Until she'd leaned in and kissed him and thrown his

equilibrium and everything he thought he knew about her out the window.

She wasn't at the bar. It was a safe bet that she'd already made it out the door.

He made it outside just as she reached her car.

"Maddie, wait." He sprinted toward her.

He was always in charge of himself. Usually, he had the upper hand with women. The bottom line was he had to so that he didn't give the women he saw the wrong idea. He had no room in his life for a relationship right now. Maybe someday, but not right now. That's why he never let it get that far. That's why he never got emotionally involved. He walked away before anything could take root. Maybe it was a chicken and egg thing. Maybe he could walk away because nothing had taken root. Not in a very long time. But that was another lifetime ago, before he was who he was now. That relationship had only reinforced the importance of not letting himself get too deeply involved. He'd learned that with his family when his folks died. His family had never been there for him.

He reached her just as she fished her keys out of her purse.

"Hey, what are you doing?"

She looked at him like he was crazy.

He should've let her go.

He should've just let her get in her car and drive away.

"I'm leaving?" she said like he was a dolt. And he was, for trying to make her stay.

He needed time to think, needed to put together the

right words. But standing there with the taste of her on his lips, he couldn't think. All he could do was feel and that was a dangerous thing.

"Don't go," he said over the merriment of a group of people who looked like they were ready to party as they made their way toward the building. She shot him a questioning look that was half surprise and half question. *What do you want from me?* She hitched her purse up onto her shoulder.

"Let's take a walk," he said. "Let's get out of here."

Night had already fallen on downtown Houston and the air had turned chilly. Maddie crossed her arms in front of her and was rubbing them.

"Are you cold?" he asked. "I wish I had a jacket to offer you. If you're uncomfortable, we don't have to walk."

She arched a brow. He read her expression to mean that the kiss had made this an uncomfortable situation. Yet here they were, neither of them acting very anxious to make an exit.

"What do you want, Zach?"

"I want to talk about what just happened in there."

She opened her mouth as if to say something, but stopped and shook her head.

"I'm sorry about that. I shouldn't have kissed you."

Now he was the one who was at a loss for words, when he should've said, *Yeah, and I shouldn't have kissed you back.*

Maddie took a step forward. "I suppose walking might help warm me up," she said over her shoulder at him.

Zach could think of several other ways that he could help her warm up, but none of them involved activities the two of them could do in public. God, that kiss really had done something to him. But it was just a kiss, he told himself.

That was the thing, though. It hadn't felt like *just a kiss*.

"Where do you want to go?" she asked when he stepped up beside her.

"Let's walk to the Paisley."

Her eyes widened for a moment, but then she visibly relaxed. "That's a great idea. It's just down the way."

"I know." He smiled at her. "It seems like neutral ground."

She nodded and locked her car with her key fob.

They were different in so many ways—she was all about family and connections, while he was a loner by nature—but they connected via business. And kissing, it seemed.

They started walking down Main Street, keeping silent and maintaining a safe distance between them until they reached the construction site.

Maddie was the one who broke the silence. "I kissed you because you said you weren't staying."

"I'm staying if I win the promotion," he said. "In all fairness, I should tell you I don't intend to lose."

"If you win, I'm not staying," she said. "So, either way, it was a goodbye kiss."

They sat down on the concrete steps leading up to the high-rise's front doors. The building looked finished on the outside, but the builder was still in the process of finishing the inside. The building was located in a popular area with lots of downtown nightlife, so a steady stream of people filed by on their way to the various clubs and restaurants.

"You'd really leave your family's business?" he asked her.

She slanted him a look. "Of course. How could I stay if my own father passes me over for a promotion? Never mind. You wouldn't understand."

She waved him away and crossed her arms.

"What makes you think that I wouldn't understand?" he challenged.

She laughed. It wasn't a condescending sound, more of a note of exasperation.

"Of course you couldn't understand. I do appreciate your attempt at empathy, but you have no idea what it's like when your father doesn't take you seriously."

She paused, but he sensed she wasn't finished. So, he let her continue.

"Everyone takes Zach McCarter seriously. All you have to do is smile and people—yes, both men and women—are putty in your hands and you can mold them and form them as you see fit. My father included. Somehow you've managed to wrap him around your little finger."

She blinked at him as if her words had surprised even herself.

"Are you finished?" he asked.

She shrugged.

"You have a point," he said. "I don't know what it's like for my father not to take me seriously. My father died when I was thirteen years old. My mother died two years later. My brother was too angry at the world or too self-absorbed to want the responsibility of raising me. So, he gave me away and let me cool my heels for the next three years in the foster care system."

Maddie's face had gone ashen. "Zach, I'm sorry. I didn't know."

"Of course you didn't know. Not many people do. It's not something I advertise, but I'm not ashamed of it either. That experience made me into the man I am today."

Maddie looked down, and for a moment the two of them sat in silence on the steps of the Paisley. The sound of people on the sidewalk in front of them, the building that would determine their future to their backs.

Why had he just told her that? He'd never shared that piece of himself with any other business associate. In fact, the only person he could remember opening up to was Sharla Grasse, the only woman who'd broken his heart. All those years ago.

"You shouldn't be ashamed of who you are," Maddie said. "You can't help it."

They were quiet again.

"So, that's another thing I didn't know about you," she said.

He nodded. "That means you're up one. You owe me one."

"Okay…" she said, drawing out the word as if she was thinking. "Something you don't know about me is I'm ashamed of myself for carrying on about my father. I must sound like an entitled brat to you."

He turned to her and shook his head. "You're human.

I can imagine how it would be to be in your shoes. It would suck. You were expecting one outcome and you were disappointed by the way your father handled it. Something I do know about you is you're a hard worker. You would be very deserving of this promotion. If—" He stopped and held up a finger as if to make a point. "Let me emphasize the word *if*—because I'm not giving up and I'm not letting up. If you get it, it will be because you earned it and not because your father handed it to you."

She started to say something, but Zach opened his fingers and held up his palm to stop her. "Something else you don't know about me is I think you have the advantage in this little contest we're in. I don't know that your father even knows it, but it's true."

She looked troubled.

"That's not true," she said.

"Maybe it's not, but I think it is. Now I'm one up on you. It's your turn to tell me something I don't know about you."

She laughed. "Well, whatever the case. Technically, that last one didn't count as a something I don't know about you. It was something you're thinking, but not something truly about you. So, I'll see you that one and raise you one. I think you're an incredibly kind, caring person. I think you have an incredible outlook and love of life despite what you've been through."

She had a small mole just below her right eye. How had he never noticed it before? It made her even more beautiful. Tonight, he'd noticed a lot of things about her he'd never taken the time to slow down and see. Those lips…those eyes…the fact that her teeth were perfect, but her nose was just slightly less than so. He drank her in greedily, wanting to commit to memory every single detail of how she looked at this very moment in the dusky May twilight, with her guard down. He wanted to lean in and kiss her—take one more taste, see if he remembered right and this time memorize how she tasted, how perfectly their mouths fit together, how the chemistry that had always buzzed between them turned into white-hot electricity when they kissed.

"Are you and your brother close now?" she asked.

The bluntness of her question pulled him off the ledge, kept him from leaning in and kissing her again. Had she sensed that was what he was about to do and searched for a question to kill the mood? If so, she'd chosen the perfect one. It was the verbal equivalent of a bucket of cold water.

"If that's too nosy, you don't have to answer," she said.

"I don't mind. No, we're not close. My brother and I haven't spoken in more than a decade."

Her brow knit into a look of concern. He could see the wheels turning.

"You're probably wondering why, if he's my only family, we're not close."

She nodded. "Yes, that's exactly what I was thinking. I mean, I come from this big, crazy, sometimes downright obnoxious family and I can't think of a single thing anyone could do that would make us estranged. If any of us had a problem that big, the other ones would lock us in a room until we'd worked it out. That is if we didn't insist on working it out ourselves."

"It's not that dramatic," Zach said. "In fact, it's actually rather anticlimactic. He never had time for me when I needed him. Once I got out and started making my way in the world we were both too busy to bother."

She squinted at him and gave her head a quick shake.

"I don't understand. Does he live in California or someplace far away?"

Zach chuckled. "Actually, he lives in Austin."

"What?" Maddie said. "You two were living in the same state and you didn't bother to get together? What are you not telling me? There has to be more to this that you're not saying."

There was, and for a solid minute he looked at her, remembering Sharla and how she'd left him after he'd unloaded his past on her. In one regard, Maddie was right. Zach knew he had a way with people. As long as he smiled and brought the sunshine, they were pretty much putty in his hands, as Maddie had said. But the minute things got too heavy, people left. People didn't like to be burdened.

"Zach, tell me. I mean, you've already told me this much. You might as well tell me the rest."

"Okay, tell me if you'd lock yourself in a room to work this one out. Before our mom died, she made my brother the beneficiary of a life insurance policy. It wasn't a lot of money, but it was enough. Enough for him to raise me. She made him promise to take care of me. Granted, he was barely of age. He didn't know anything about raising a punk teenage kid who was skipping school and getting into trouble. When things got too heavy for him to handle, and child services started poking around, telling him he could be held legally responsible for my truancy, he let them take me and put me in foster care."

Zach shook his head bitterly. "He said it was for the best. He was trying to put himself through college. When I asked about the money, he said after he got through law school, he'd put me through college if I kept my nose clean. There was always an *if*...and there was always a reason why it was never a good time to make good on his promise. He had too many bills, he was getting married, his kids needed braces. But the truth was he had his career and his family and his boat and fancy car. His lifestyle had probably expanded to the outer limits of his income, but he never made good on that promise. He took the money our mother left us and ran."

Maddie was looking at him as if he'd confessed his brother was an extraterrestrial. "How could he do that?"

"It sounds really sordid, doesn't it?" He hated her look of pity. "I don't know why I unloaded all that on you."

"Zach, you needed to tell someone. I'm sorry that happened to you."

He waved her off. "You don't need to be sorry. I've obviously done all right for myself. I asked him for help. He wasn't in the position to do it. It was fine. Like I said, fending for myself made me the person I am today. So, it's all good. No need to worry about me."

Except that he wanted to pull her into his arms and taste her lips again. She should worry about that.

Her kiss had unleashed a need in him that was proving difficult to ignore. He wanted to lean in and kiss her again. Hell, that wasn't all he wanted to do.

If Maddie knew what was good for her, she'd stay far away from him.

They'd had a moment. That was all.

They'd kissed and it couldn't be undone.

After she and Zach had parted ways the night before, Maddie had made a pit stop at the Kroger where she'd purchased a package of Oreo cookies and a pint of Ben & Jerry's Cherry Garcia, which she'd opted for over her usual go-to flavor, Half Baked, because it seemed to mock the very problem that had driven her to the junk food in the first place.

What kind of a half-baked notion had made her think it was a good idea to kiss Zach McCarter?

He'd been so nice to her afterward, too. Her heart thudded hard against her breastbone as she remembered the tenderness in his gaze. At one point, she'd wondered if he might kiss her again. Against all that was sane and good, she'd wanted him to. But he didn't.

Which was both the best and worst thing that could have happened.

Why did he have to be so nice? Especially after he'd suffered his own hardships? Why couldn't he have acted like a jackass and tried to move in for more? She would've put a stop to it in a big hurry. Or why couldn't he at least have let her walk away so she could've gone home and eaten her feelings in that emergency first aid of ice cream and cookies? If he would've let her walk away, she would've driven away feeling self-righteously superior that her suspicions about him had been confirmed: he was a player and a scoundrel, a wheeler-dealer who wasn't interested in her and only interested in winning.

Instead, he'd been concerned about her. He'd confessed her father's arrangement had surprised him as much as it had surprised her. For a few moments after they'd parted, she'd wondered if his confession had been a ploy, a means to play her by making her feel sorry for him. The rich girl would still have opportunities if she didn't get the promotion, but the poor man—though, now he wasn't a poor man by any means—was simply reaping the rewards of a life of hard work.

If he was trying to play her, he was being subtle. If he was being sincere, it was so sad to think that he had a brother to whom he hadn't spoken in over a decade. Sometimes men could be so stubborn. Surely, Zach wouldn't have made up a story about what drove him and his brother apart. But if they were each other's only family, and both of them were doing well, couldn't they sit down and talk things out? Sure, it was easy for her to play armchair referee. She'd been raised with every advantage, but even if the worst happened and her father hired Zach over her, even if she left Fortunado to start up her own venture, which she most certainly would do if it came to that, she would not allow it to drive a wedge between her and her dad. Nothing was worth more than family.

She couldn't stop thinking about what Zach had said about his brother.

His name was Rich and he was an attorney in Austin. She turned on the desktop computer in her home office. When it was fully booted, she searched for Richard McCarter, attorney.

The first item the search engine offered was the law offices of McCarter and Black.

Bingo.

Rich was easy to pick out of a photo of the firm's partners. He was a slightly older, less handsome version of Zach. Zach had obviously been the brother who had been blessed with the lion's share of the handsome genes. Not that Rich wasn't handsome.

There was another photo—a family photo used for an ad for Richard McCarter's run for city council—a failed bid, a bit more research showed. Even so, it showed him smiling up from a blue picnic blanket that was spread out beneath an ancient oak tree. A pretty brunette and three kids who looked to be in elementary and middle school surrounded him. For all intents and purposes, he looked like the quintessential family man. Of course, anyone could portray themselves however they wanted in a staged photo, but at face value, the guy looked like his family was important to him.

If so, how could he shut out his brother?

A plan was forming in the outer reaches of her mind. Lately, she'd been coming up with a lot of half-baked ideas—believing her father would promote her without making her jump through hoops, kissing Zach... Oh, yes, she seemed to be full of foolish ideas lately. What was one more, especially if she could help reunite a family? Yes, a definite plan was starting to take shape. Maybe she could play mediator to get Zach and his brother talking again.

A lot could change in a decade.

As she prepared to go over to her parents' house to meet her sisters—Carlo was out of town this weekend and Schuyler was driving in to spend a couple of days with family—she started scheming. She needed to go back to Austin for the closing of Carlo and Schuyler's house. They'd put in an offer on the mini Spanish castle overlooking Lake Austin and the seller had accepted it. Since it was a cash sale, they were due to close next week, right before the wedding. And she needed to show them more commercial properties to consider for the nightclub. While she was there, she might just have to pay Rich McCarter a visit and assess the damage.

More immediately, she needed to prepare herself to see her father. She needed to have a new mind-set. Today, she would put aside her wounded pride and re-double her determination to win the promotion. Sitting around feeling sorry for herself wasn't going to do her any good.

For that matter, neither was boycotting her favorite Ben & Jerry's ice cream flavor. The Cherry Garcia was delicious, of course, but not nearly as satisfying as Half Baked. This morning, as she tossed the empty ice-cream pint into the trash and sequestered the remaining Oreos in a zippered plastic bag, she was feeling bloated and unsatisfied, with a craving for cookie dough and brownie bites—and another taste of Zach.

She set the bag of cookies next to her purse so she wouldn't forget to take them to her parents' house, where she, Val and Schuyler were converging for a sisters' weekend. She seriously considered another Kroger stop before meeting them. They deserved ice cream—even though Schuyler had been last-minute wedding dieting.

Maddie put her hand on her stomach. To nip that temptation in the bud, she plucked the pint out of the trash and surveyed the nutritional panel.

After adding up the caloric count, she dropped the container like it was burning her fingers. Nearly five hundred calories and an entire day's worth of fat grams in one pitiful pity-party-for-one. And that didn't include the Oreos.

Zach's kiss had been much sweeter.

She blinked away the thought and reminded herself that she'd have to work out extra hard on Monday since she wouldn't have time to hit the gym this weekend. It would be good to have an outlet for her pent-up emotions.

Zach McCarter didn't stand a chance.

"Bring it on," she murmured to Ramona, her two-year-old corgi, who had padded into the kitchen and was leaning against Maddie's leg as if showing her solidarity. Maddie leaned down and scratched the little dog behind her ear. The animal stared up at her with soulful eyes as if trying to understand what she was saying.

"I know," Maddie said. "The whole thing doesn't make any sense to me either. What can I do other than give it my best shot?"

The dog plopped down on top of Maddie's foot. "At least I know you're on my side, Ramona. But we must go now. You're coming with me to Grandma's house. We're going to spend some time with Aunt Schuyler and Aunt Val. Doesn't that sound like fun?"

Maddie gently extricated her foot and bent down to give the little dog one more scratch, relishing the silky softness of her velvety sienna ear before attaching the leash. Ramona gazed up at her lovingly. Maddie grabbed her purse and the bag of Oreos and headed out the door.

Chapter Five

Forty-five minutes later, Maddie got out of her white Volvo, smoothed her yellow sundress and walked around to the passenger side to free Ramona from her doggie seat belt, and fetch her parcels. A small bag contained her dog's food, dishes, treats and toys, and another larger shopping bag contained the bag of Oreos and a dozen assorted cupcakes from Moonbeam Bakery, the home of Houston's most delicious baked goods. She'd resisted a Ben & Jerry's run, but this occasion called for cupcakes.

Val's car wasn't in the driveway yet, but Schuyler's sleek red BMW was parked front and center and Maddie smiled at the thought of having some sister time. Since Schuyler had moved to Austin and she and Val worked so darn much, times like this were fewer and farther between.

Seriously, when was the last time she'd taken an entire Saturday off? Even though she intended to win the promotion, the pragmatic side of her wondered if maybe this episode with Zach and the promotion was the universe's way to teach her about balance. Really, she couldn't go on the way she'd been going. It made her realize that if all the material things were stripped away, what would she have? She'd have her family, of course, but her parents were prepping for the second chapter of their lives and her little sister was getting married.

Forty years down the road did she want to be Crazy Old Aunt Maddie? Did she want her siblings and future nieces and nephews whispering about her behind her back, calling her the spinster sister?

No.

In that spirit, today would be about fun. As she closed the distance between the driveway and the grand front porch, her phone pinged, alerting her that a new message had come in. Reflexively, she glanced at it as she walked toward the huge wooden double doors of her parents' home, but resisted checking it. She had her hands full with precious cargo. She certainly didn't want to upset the cupcakes before her sisters had a chance to ooh and aah over the little works of art, and gripe and curse her for bringing them because they were trying to diet.

But in the end, they'd eat them—between the four of them—Schuyler, Val, their mother and herself, they'd probably polish them off.

She might even offer one to her dad to prove she harbored no ill feelings over the Zach situation.

Liar.

She braced herself for the likelihood that before the weekend was through, she and her sisters would probably ponder how their father could, in his right mind, consider turning the family business over to Zach. It would feel good to have them rally around her.

But she wouldn't tell them she'd kissed Zach. Because she probably wouldn't be able to fashion a poker face that didn't betray how much she'd loved that kiss.

If the girls started dissing Zach and their dad too much, she would remind them that this was in her power. She had this. She wouldn't allow their dad to turn the company over to Zach or anyone else who wasn't part of the family. It suddenly dawned on her that maybe this whole competition was nothing but a charade. Her father's way of posing one last challenge.

She breathed in the sweet smell of a sunny spring day and redoubled her determination to accept this situation for what it was: one last hoop for her to jump through, manufactured by Kenneth Fortunado before he turned loose his life's work for a life of leisure.

She couldn't stop thinking of how Zach and his brother had let money come between them. Even if her own pride was hurt by the way her father had handled things, Maddie put herself in his shoes. She knew turning over the company had to be hard for her dad. A wave of sympathy tenderized the anger she'd been chewing on all week. Letting go of his empire wasn't easy. She couldn't—or at least she shouldn't—blame him for flexing his power muscles one more time. In the effort of being a good daughter, she would not only give him this, she would prove to him that he had nothing to worry about.

Maddie let herself and Ramona in the front door and followed the sound of voices and puppy barks.

"Fluff and Stuff are here!" Maddie told her dog. "Are you excited to play with your cousins?" Ramona answered with an excited bark and quickened her pace, her nails clicking on the hardwood floors as she trotted toward the kitchen. That's where she found her mother and Schuyler seated at the marble island with a bunch of brochures spread out in front of them. Schuyler's puppies played rough-and-tumble on the expansive kitchen floor.

The little dogs stopped their acrobatics as they sensed Ramona enter the room. Soon the three dogs were happily chasing each other around like long-lost friends.

Unfortunately, the same air of goodwill wasn't flowing between Schuyler and Barbara. In fact, the tension was nearly palpable and Maddie quickly realized they were engaged in a lively debate about wedding flowers.

"I really think we should scrap the orchids and opt for extra peonies," their mother said. "Peonies will hold up much better than orchids. They're so fragile. You don't want your flowers to be drooping before you walk down the aisle."

"But I like the clean, simple look of orchids. It completely changes my vision if we don't have orchids. Peonies are so froufrou."

"Hi," Maddie said. Both women turned toward her.

"Hi, honey," Barbara said. "I'm glad you're here. And where is my little granddog Ramona?"

Ramona yipped and broke away from the pack only long enough to put her front paws on Barbara's leg. Barbara reached down and gave her a loving scratch behind the ears.

Ramona seemed like a welcome distraction, even if it was just momentary. "Schuyler and I were just putting the finishing touches on the flowers for the wedding," Barbara said. "Come in and tell us your thoughts."

The wedding was right around the corner. Schuyler and their mother were past the point of fun and ready for the big day to get here. Reading between the lines, Maddie knew what her mother really meant was, *Come in and be the tiebreaker.*

Where was Val when she needed her?

"My knowledge of flowers is basically roses are red, violets are blue," Maddie said. "Although, I always thought violets were purple. But maybe that proves that I'm a disaster when it comes to color or at the very least I'm color-blind."

"You are not a disaster when it comes to color," her mother said. "As a matter of fact, you're very good at it. Look at all those homes you've staged and sold. If that's not proof, then I don't know what is. I've been telling your father that." Barbara arched her brows. Her expression made it clear that she did not approve of the way her husband had handled things. Of course, Barbara Fortunado was a mama bear personified. She couldn't stand to see her babies hurt, and it gave Maddie a great deal of satisfaction to know that her mother was on her side.

Her mother never shied away from voicing her opinion—
like with Schuyler's wedding flowers—but when it came
to things that involved her kids, she was also their best
advocate. Fiercely loyal, she would go to the mat for her
babies. If Maddie knew her mother as well as she believed she did, Barbara probably hadn't minced words
when she'd voiced her disapproval to her husband. However, Barbara was also a Southern lady. Southern ladies
did not talk ill of their husbands to anyone—especially
not to their daughters.

"Come in." Barbara's stool scraped the hardwood
kitchen floor as she pushed it away and stood. She took
the cupcakes and Oreos out of Maddie's hands, un-
bagged them, and placed them on the island.

The zippered bag of cookies seemed to scream that
Maddie had recently binged. For a second she contemplated pretending like she'd brought them as a garnish
and sticking one in each of the cupcakes' fluffy icing.
But she wasn't sure Oreo would go with the various fla-
vors. No, she was better off leaving well enough alone.

She was a connoisseur, not Martha Stewart. She
knew her strengths and her limits, and that was a
strength she was proud of.

"Sit down," her mother told her. "Try some of these
stuffed mushrooms and brisket-wrapped asparagus that
the caterer sent all the way from Austin with Schuyler
for us to try."

Schuyler and Carlo were getting married in the
sculpture garden at the Mendoza Winery in Austin,
which Carlo and his cousins had purchased last year.
The reception would be catered by La Viña, the win-

ery's restaurant that overlooked the vineyard. It would be a stunning evening.

Maddie's heart twisted. She was so happy for her sister and she didn't begrudge her one single second of the happiness she'd found with Carlo and the thrill of feeling like a princess as she planned this once-in-a-lifetime event. But since her father had dropped the bomb, Maddie had to admit, beneath the anger, she'd discovered a gaping hole. Something was missing from her life and when she saw how happy and complete Schuyler looked after meeting the love of her life, Maddie wanted the same for herself.

Or at least she did in theory. In reality, allowing herself to lose control and fall in love was a scary prospect.

"All the way from Austin, huh?" Maddie asked.

Schuyler nodded. "They sent them in one of those insulated bags so they'd stay warm. I think they're delicious. What does my maid of honor think?"

"They look fabulous," Maddie said and helped herself to a mushroom.

"Let me fix you a glass of iced tea." Barbara was fussing over her just a little too much. It made Maddie wonder if her mom was overcompensating for her dad's promotion challenge. Kenneth Fortunado might be the head of his real estate empire, but there was no mistake that Barbara ruled the roost at home. Maddie wished she could've been a fly on the wall when her mother had first heard the news. Although Barbara was never one to interfere in her husband's business matters, she held an MBA and was an astute businesswoman in her own right. She ran the Fortunado Foundation, working with the financial gurus who oversaw the nonprofit's vast portfolio and beneficiaries, which mostly consisted of women and children.

"How are you, honey?" Concern was etched on Barbara's face as she slid a large glass of tea, complete with lemon round and mint sprig, in front of Maddie, who was still standing. "Are you doing okay?"

"I'm fine, Mom." Maddie squared her shoulders and smiled as if she hadn't noticed her mother's pained look. "How are you?"

She bit into a spear of asparagus.

"Just fine, sweetheart. I'm so happy to have all my girls here today. Or at least we will be once Val arrives."

Maddie nodded. "These are great, Sky. I vote yes on both."

Barbara was peering at her with a look that registered somewhere between motherly concern and tiptoeing on eggshells. It was as if she might be able to spot the crack in Maddie's facade if she looked closely enough. But all cracks and bruises had been carefully patched and concealed. Her mother would be hard-pressed to detect even a hint of damage.

Schuyler seemed oblivious to her mother's delicate questioning.

"Whatcha got there, Mads?" she asked, eyeing the items their mom had placed on the granite island.

"Cookies and Moonbeam Bakery cupcakes." Maddie reached for the box and slid it down to her sister.

Schuyler held up her fingers in the sign of the cross. "You she-devil! Keep those cupcakes away from me.

You know I'm trying to diet so I can fit into my wedding gown. How could you?"

"If you lose any more weight, your wedding gown is going to fall off," Maddie said. "Come on, Sky, it's a girls' weekend. We deserve a treat."

"Yes, we do," Barbara said, as she untied the light blue ribbon with the trademark white stars. Their mother lifted the lid and inhaled deeply. "My, oh, my, they smell good. I call dibs on the sweet tea cake with lemon icing."

Schuyler scrunched up her nose. "And you brought us a half-eaten package of cookies? Are the Moonbeam cupcakes just a Trojan horse to hide the fact that you're trying to unload all your leftover sweets on us?"

"No, Schuyler." Maddie flashed a mischievous smile at her sister. "You don't have to eat them. There will be more for us, right, Mom?"

Except, that was exactly why she'd brought the cookies to her parents' house, to get them out of her own house.

Schuyler reached over and helped herself to a cookie. She separated it, exposing the creamy center, which she scraped with her teeth.

"Save some for the rest of us," Maddie chided, snatching one for herself.

"Girls," their mom reprimanded.

Even though this was the way Maddie and her sister had always communicated—they gently sparred—they didn't mean anything bad by it. They certainly didn't wish each other any harm. They were simply as different as the tortoise and the hare—in every regard—and this was one of the ways they celebrated their differences.

"Maddie, why don't you put the cookies and cupcakes on a plate?" Barbara reached into the cabinet and pulled out a colorful ceramic platter she'd purchased in Italy on one of the rare vacations she'd managed to coerce her husband into taking. She handed it to her daughter, who prepared to do as her mother suggested.

"Where's Carlo this weekend?" Maddie asked, happy to change the subject.

"He's in Napa this weekend, taking care of some vineyard business before the wedding."

A quip about when Dad was going to meet with Carlo to arrange the final payoff for his agreeing to marry Schuyler played through Maddie's head. Even though it was meant as good-natured teasing, she stopped short of saying it because it might sound mean. As much as she and her sister loved to banter, Maddie feared that would cross the line. At worst, it might hurt Schuyler's feelings; at best it might make Maddie look jealous. And she was. Sort of. Well, not the begrudging type of jealous, simply the type that wished she had someone who loved her as much as Carlo loved Schuyler.

"Napa?" Maddie echoed. "I'm surprised that you didn't go with him. Napa is gorgeous this time of year."

"It's always gorgeous," Schuyler said, "and there will be plenty of opportunities for us to visit in the future, but this might be my last chance for a sisters' weekend while I'm still single."

Schuyler had made it clear that instead of a party-hard bachelorette party, she wanted a nice, quiet pampering weekend with her sisters.

It suddenly dawned on Maddie that *this* was that weekend.

Had she been so self-absorbed that she'd nearly forgotten her sister's bachelorette party? God love Schuyler for being willing to meet her halfway—and with such a good nature, too. Her sister had taken it upon herself to show up. The least she could do was provide the bachelorette weekend of her sister's dreams.

At that moment, they heard Val sing, "Hello!" from the hallway. Like magic, she appeared with a bouquet of pink and gold balloons and a shopping bag from the liquor store.

"Where's my favorite bride-to-be?" she said. "Are you ready for a sisters' weekend of a lifetime?"

Val set down the bag and fished out a beauty pageant–type sash that aptly said *Bride-To-Be* in gold glitter, along with a plastic tiara with rhinestones and a strip of baby pink marabou at the base. Schuyler squealed.

"Let's get this party started," Val said. "I brought the champagne. And I got us fancy glasses."

Val set out four bottles of Veuve Clicquot rosé and four painted wine goblets, that were customized to each of the women present.

Schuyler's, of course, said *Bride-To-Be*. Their mother's glass said *MOB Boss*—MOB meaning mother of the bride. Maddie's was Maid of Honor, but should've said *Self-absorbed Slacker*; and Val's said *Favorite Sister*.

Not only did Val deserve that title, but Maddie wanted to add *Goddess* and *Lifesaver*. Her little sister

Dear Reader,

IT'S A FACT: if you answer 4 quick questions, we'll send you 4 FREE REWARDS!

I'm not kidding you. As a leading publisher of women's fiction, we value your opinions... and your time. That's why we are prepared to **reward** you handsomely for completing our mini-survey. In fact, we have 4 Free Rewards for you, including 2 free books and 2 free gifts.

As you may have guessed, that's why our mini-survey is called **"4 for 4".** Answer 4 questions and get 4 Free Rewards. It's that simple!

Thank you for participating in our survey,

Pam Powers

To get your 4 FREE REWARDS:
Complete the survey below and return the insert today to receive 2 FREE BOOKS and 2 FREE GIFTS guaranteed!

"4 for 4" MINI-SURVEY

1 Is reading one of your favorite hobbies?
☐ YES ☐ NO

2 Do you prefer to read instead of watch TV?
☐ YES ☐ NO

3 Do you read newspapers and magazines?
☐ YES ☐ NO

4 Do you enjoy trying new book series with FREE BOOKS?
☐ YES ☐ NO

YES! I have completed the above Mini-Survey. Please send me my 4 FREE REWARDS (worth over $20 retail). I understand that I am under no obligation to buy anything, as explained on the back of this card.

235/335 HDL GMYE

FIRST NAME	LAST NAME

ADDRESS

APT.#	CITY

STATE/PROV.	ZIP/POSTAL CODE

READER SERVICE—Here's how it works:

had saved the day and she was making it appear that she and Maddie had planned everything this way.

She was humbled. Even though she hadn't forgotten Schuyler's visit, she had been so caught up in her own issues that she'd been failing on her maid of honor duties. But Val—fabulous, wonderful Val—had quietly picked up the slack.

Maybe she didn't have it as together as she thought. Maybe she still needed to grow a little bit—rather than being fully formed and perfectly ready to step into the Fortunado president's role. If she could forget her sister's bachelorette party, she needed to take a step back and see what else she was missing. But not now. She'd already spent too much time focused inward. She wasn't going to do that this weekend. But she did file away an urgent mandate to do some serious inventory at the beginning of the week.

Schuyler opened the first bottle of sparkling rosé with a loud *pop* of the cork. It caused the champagne to foam up out of the bottle and spill down over the neck.

"Oh, Schuyler," Barbara good-naturedly reprimanded. "Let me get a dishcloth to clean up that mess."

"No, Mom," Maddie said. "You relax. I'll get it."

Barbara put a hand on her oldest daughter's shoulder. "Oh, honey. Let me do it. You've been working so hard with all that your father has put on you this week."

Maddie silenced her mother with a nearly imperceptible shake of her head. Thank goodness, the astute woman caught on. The last thing they needed right now was for the attention to be diverted from Schuyler to the race for the Fortunado presidency. The last thing

Maddie wanted to deal with right now was Schuyler peppering her with questions about Zach.

Too late.

"Speaking of working hard," Schuyler said. "How's everything with Zach? Have you two had that Ping-Pong date yet?"

"No, we haven't." Maddie kept her voice light. "Is there anything special you want to do this weekend, Sky?"

"I swung by the Thirsty Ox last night," Val said as she gave her sister a knowing look. "I saw that you and Zach were the only ones from our usual group. So, I didn't stay. The two of you looked pretty intense."

Val arched a brow before she picked up the bottle and started serving the champagne.

Val had seen them? *Oh, crap. What else did she see?*

And why was she bringing it up? She was in dire danger of losing her "favorite sister" status if she wasn't careful.

"So, you and Zach were getting intense at the Thirsty Ox last night?" Schuyler's mouth fell open and her eyes were huge and greedy.

"Yes, a bunch of us always go there for happy hour on Friday nights." Maddie shrugged it off like it was no big deal and let her gaze fall to her mother who was mopping up the spilled pink champagne and watching the scene unfold like she had a ringside seat at the roller derby.

"But it was just you and Zach. And Val says you were getting intense." Schuyler raised an eyebrow. "What exactly does that mean, Mads? And more important, is there something brewing that we should know about? Come on, Maddie. Spill it. I'm the bride-to be. This is my party. I demand to know."

Oh, there was something brewing, all right. Only, not in the way her sister was insinuating.

An emotional storm was brewing. A storm of gargantuan proportions. If Val saw her kissing Zach—and judging by how coy she was acting, Maddie had a sinking feeling she had seen them—Maddie predicted there might be some squalls this weekend.

"Calm down, Bridezilla." Maddie rolled her eyes at her sister. "I've already told you he's not my type."

Schuyler scrunched up her pretty face. "Well, okay. Since you brought it up, what *is* your type, Mads?"

"My type doesn't really matter because I haven't even had time to think about what my type would be." *Liar. It's Zach.* "Even if I knew, I'm too busy working to date."

"I don't buy that." Schuyler squinted at Maddie.

Maddie shrugged. "Sorry to disappoint you, but that's my life right now. I'm happy for you and Carlo. You found each other. You're going to marry the love of your life and that's great. But you know what, Sky? I'm perfectly happy with my life the way it is."

Double liar. Maddie purposely avoided eye contact with her mother since the woman sometimes possessed the uncanny ability to read her mind.

"But you're bringing a date to the wedding, right?" Schuyler was undeterred.

"Probably not." She took a bite of her cookie.

"Why not?"

"Did you not hear what I just said? I'm not bringing just anyone to a family wedding and I certainly don't have time to go out and meet someone now."

"You should ask Zach," Schuyler said.

The way Maddie's breath hitched at the suggestion made her swallow wrong and choke on her cookie.

Barbara clapped Maddie on the back.

"Mom, I'm fine. I just—" Another round of coughing preempted Maddie's words.

"Here." Barbara thrust her glass of sparkling rosé at Maddie. "Drink this."

Grateful for the diversion, Maddie took the champagne and took a long swallow. The bubbles tickled her nose and burned the back of her throat, making her eyes water.

"Gosh, I didn't mean to get you all choked up," Schuyler said. "Who knew that the mere mention of Zach McCarter would do that."

As Maddie blinked away the moisture that had gathered in her eyes during her coughing fit, a stifling heat settled around her. It had her pulling at her dress and trying to ignore the way the searing heat burned her cheeks.

"Even more reason that you should bring him as your date to the wedding," Schuyler said.

"And on that note," Maddie said, "I think we need to have a toast."

Barbara jumped up. "And after that I'll just go put these extra bottles in the spare refrigerator. I wouldn't want them to get warm."

The Fortunado women held up their glasses. "To a

fun weekend together," Maddie said, trying to infuse enough happiness into her voice that it would sway them to change the subject. "And to family, the most important thing in the world."

After they clinked glasses, Barbara snagged an Oreo off the plate and popped it into her mouth. Before she grabbed the unopened three bottles and walked out of the kitchen, she turned to her daughters. "You girls behave yourself. And, Schuyler, eat a cupcake and don't bully your sister about bringing a date. This may be your weekend, but it doesn't give you a license to abandon your manners."

Maddie could have kissed her mom. She loved her sister, but sometimes Schuyler had a one-track mind. Like a bulldog with a bone, she could latch onto things and not give up. Case in point: Schuyler was happily engaged to Carlo Mendoza and therefore thought everyone should be as happily in love as she and Carlo.

Nice idea in theory, but not exactly practical for the rest of the nonromantics of the world. But you might as well speak Latin to Schuyler instead of trying to explain this concept. She couldn't seem to comprehend that not everyone was destined to meet their soul mate.

If only.

Barbara had no more than cleared the kitchen when Schuyler set down her glass and turned to Maddie.

"I know you've been super busy with work. But you're free this weekend." Schuyler's eyes had a certain glint that scared Maddie.

"No, I'm not free. It's your bachelorette party. It's

our sisters' weekend. I'm very busy—we are going to be busy—and I wouldn't have it any other way."

She would be crazy busy next week working a whole lot more since it was the final week to put the finishing touch on the Paisley proposal and reel in the deal so she could secure her future.

"I know that," Schuyler said. "And I appreciate that you're devoting a whole weekend to me when you have so much on your plate. So, I'm going to make it extra simple for you. You know what I want to do tonight?"

"I'm afraid to ask, but I have a feeling you're about to tell us."

"You're darn right I am." Schuyler knocked back the champagne that was in her glass and held it out for Val to pour some more. "I want to play Ping-Pong tonight."

Oh, no, she wasn't—

"And I want one gorgeous guy to come over and play with us."

Schuyler bit her bottom lip and looked as if she might explode with delight as she milked the situation for all it was worth.

"Val, would you be a sweetheart and call Zach McCarter and ask him to join us tonight?"

"Maddie brought cupcakes." Schuyler thrust the open box at Zach, and Maddie wanted to hide under the Ping-Pong table. "Try one."

"I'd love to sample your sweets," he said, his eyes locking with Maddie's, and damned if she didn't feel the heat flood her cheeks again.

It was a game to him.

Well, two could play that game.

"Right here? In my parents' house? Aren't you brave."

She held his gaze and watched him mentally back-pedal.

Sort of.

"I never have been able to resist a good cupcake. How did you know they were my favorite?"

She couldn't take her eyes off his as he bit into it. She hated herself for melting just a little on the inside. And, wow, nice of her sisters to be so facilitating. Calling him up and somehow persuading him to drop everything to come over for cupcakes and Ping-Pong. Were they in middle school?

Maddie glanced at them, but they were pretending to be engrossed in a conversation of their own.

After what transpired last night, this was possibly the most awkward situation she'd been in in a long time. She didn't know whether to curse her sisters for making it happen or pledge her undying gratitude.

This was either the beginning of something disastrous…or something very, very good.

Chapter Six

"Ready to get down to business?" Zach asked after he'd finished his cupcake—dark chocolate with mocha icing. "Best three of five? Winner of each round is the person who reaches ten first."

Standing in the Fortunado recreation room, staring across the long green tennis table at Maddie, Zach couldn't imagine any place else he'd rather be right now. Even with Schuyler and Val sitting on the sidelines, lost in conversation about who knew what, not really paying attention.

"Sure." Maddie grimaced at Schuyler. "The winner can play the guest of honor."

Schuyler pointedly stared at Val, acting completely engrossed in their conversation.

When Val had called him and extended the invitation to come over—to play Ping-Pong, of all things—he wondered if this was a setup orchestrated by the sisters on behalf of Maddie. What had she told them? He'd had other plans, but he had immediately rescheduled them.

Why not? He hadn't engaged in a good round of table tennis in years. It seemed like a good way to break the ice after the events of the previous night. Even if Maddie's sisters had in mind a personal outcome for Maddie and him, he would steer this get-together another way. It would be a fun, nonthreatening way to get him and Maddie back on the business track. They were meeting with Dave Madison, the developer of the Paisley, first thing Monday morning. It would be a good opportunity to go over their strategy so that their Monday meeting with Madison would be seamless and, most important, successful. They had one week before the wedding, one week before Kenneth would make his decision.

"You serve first." Zach tossed the ball across the table to Maddie. She caught it with a deft swipe of her left hand and proceeded to bounce the ball on the table with the paddle, showing off her skills.

Maddie was quieter than usual. Almost to the point of seeming that she didn't want him there. Zach was feeling a little subdued himself. That was even more reason that they needed to get over the quicksand of awkwardness and back on stable ground. He was happy to be the one to lead the way.

"Now you're just showing off." Zach picked up the beer Schuyler had offered him when he'd arrived. "Where are your parents?"

"They're out tonight." She rolled her eyes. "Disappointed that you won't get to try to score some personal points with Daddy?"

"No, just having flashbacks to high school," he said. "Playing Ping-Pong and drinking beer while the parents are out."

"Is that how you spent your Saturday nights?" Maddie asked.

"Embarrassingly, yes. Quite a few."

They laughed.

"So, you were a nerd, Zach?" she said.

"Be careful how you toss around that word," he said. "I seem to remember someone saying your past is steeped in the game, too."

"I love nerd couples," Schuyler said from the sidelines.

Both Zach's and Maddie's heads swiveled to look at her.

"Schuyler." Maddie glared at her sister. "Can you not?"

Ah, so there was an ulterior motive.

Zach didn't hate the idea.

He hadn't been completely immune to that kiss. If he was honest, it had taken everything in his power to stop himself from leaning in and kissing her again.

He'd woken up this morning thinking about that kiss and—

"Prepare to be annihilated, McCarter."

A second after the warning, Maddie served, sending the ball over the net with lightning-quick precision. He barely had time to raise his paddle before it bounced off the edge of the table.

"One, zip," Maddie said.

"Hey, I thought we were both supposed to be ready before we started," Zach protested as he put down his beer, retrieved the ball and rolled it across the table to her.

"McCarter, I'm always ready. I thought you were, too. Obviously, I was mistaken."

"You're always ready," Zach repeated. "That's one of the things I like about you."

"Let's get this over with," she said, making the ball dance with several whacks of the paddle.

"Do you have somewhere you need to be?" he asked, noting the edge in her voice.

"Tonight is my sister's bachelorette party. The last thing I planned on doing was playing a match of Ping-Pong with you."

She really didn't want to be here. She didn't want him there either. "The last thing, huh? Well, at least I was on your list, even if I was the last thing."

She shot him a perplexed look. "I have no idea what you're talking about. I planned a party. You weren't invited."

She leaned forward to launch her second serve and a hint of cleavage peeked out of her top. Zach tore his eyes away.

"Ouch," he said, returning the ball like he meant business. "That's mean. Do you want me to leave?" They volleyed several rounds. "When Val invited me over, I didn't realize you had other plans. I'll go."

Maddie looked up and the ball she'd returned hit the net.

"I always finish what I start," she said.

"Do you?" He gave her a knowing look and her cheeks flushed a pretty shade of pink.

She lifted her chin a notch. "Always. Your serve."

The raw look in her eyes coupled with the memory of her kiss made him imagine exactly how they might finish that kiss. If they were going to finish what they'd started, it would have to go a lot further than a kiss.

He answered by slamming the ball across the table. She returned it with equal force.

Innuendo was not the way to get them back on steady business ground. He tried a more direct approach.

"I had lunch with Dave Madison today."

Maddie missed the ball, but rather than going after it, she set down her paddle on the table. "He's out of town. How could you have had lunch with him?"

"He got back last night. Dave and I go way back."

She put her hands on her hips. Zach noticed that somewhere along the way, Val and Schuyler had left the room. "You didn't tell me you're BFFs with Dave Madison."

"I don't know if I'd go so far as to call him my BFF."

"Quit being flippant."

"I'd say calling Dave my BFF has quite a bit of *flip* to it."

"Why didn't you tell me, Zach? Why were you keeping that little tidbit to yourself?"

"I just told you."

"Did you know this last night?"

"I did."

"You kissed me and you didn't bother to inform me

you were meeting with Dave or, even better, invite me to join you?"

"If I recall, you were the one who initiated the kiss."

Her cheeks flushed again, but this time her eyes flashed. "Don't change the subject. Zach, we promised that we were going to work together on this project. Withholding information like that is not working together. I think you should go."

"I think we need to sit down and talk about this before we meet on Monday. If not, we're not going to bring our A game."

"I wanted to trust you, but I guess you're no better than anyone else who is out for himself. So much for working together."

Reading between the lines, he could take her *no better than anyone else* comment as she was comparing him to his brother, Rich. She didn't say it, but the suggestion was there. Or maybe that was still a tender spot with him. Either way—whether she was stealthily punching below the belt or he was drawing his own conclusion—it stung. He should've never confided in her—or anyone—but mostly her. Because for some reason, Maddie Fortunado made him feel emotionally vulnerable in a way he hadn't felt in years.

Why else would he have come over here so eagerly, rearranging his Saturday evening plans so he could see her under the guise of an asinine game like Ping-Pong?

"It's two-one," Zach said. "If you quit now, I win. You'll owe me five *one things*."

"Because this is all just a game to you, isn't it?" She

looked him up and down and he'd never felt so naked and exposed. Was that how she saw him?

"Fine, Zach. You win. That's all you wanted. It seems to be the only thing that's important to you."

It's not the only *thing.*

She started to walk out of the room.

"Maddie, stop. Come back, please. I didn't tell you because I knew you would want to come."

She whirled around. The intensity of her glare nearly leveled him.

"Wow. Thanks for that, Zach." Her voice dripped with sarcasm. "I feel so much better now that I know your true intentions."

"That's out of context. Let me finish."

He looked up at the ceiling, trying to gather his thoughts. Never had a woman had the ability to rattle him like she did. He prided himself on being unshakable. How the hell did she do that?

Why the hell are you letting her do it?

"Dave and I go way back. I knew him from Dallas when I was there. Long before I started working for Fortunado. I wanted to use this lunch to ease into the subject of us taking over as the exclusive listing agents for the Paisley. If you would've come, it would've obviously been a business lunch. You and I are work associates. What was I supposed to say? 'This is Maddie Fortunado. She and I want your business?' It wasn't that kind of lunch. I couldn't bring you. It's not like you're my girlfriend."

The nanosecond the words left his mouth, he knew he'd put his foot in it deep.

Jackass.

"No, I'm not your girlfriend," Maddie said. "Let's just get that straight right now. I'm sure I have absolutely nothing in common with the women you date. Therefore, you and I have nothing in common beyond work. You bring your A game on Monday and I'll bring mine. We should be perfectly fine. Goodbye, Zach."

She wasn't his girlfriend. If it hadn't been clear before, it was perfectly clear now. And so was the fact that she had embarrassed herself by kissing him.

Every time she thought she had the upper hand, Zach surprised her and came out of nowhere with a better, stronger plan.

Case in point: his clandestine lunchtime meeting with Dave Madison.

"I still can't believe you made him leave," Schuyler said as they sat in the living room after Zach's departure. "Val and I left you two alone so you could get cozy, not so you could pick a fight and kick him out."

"I had a good reason for kicking him out," Maddie said, rubbing a rough spot on one of her fingernails.

Schuyler swatted her hand. "Stop picking at your nails. Forget that I'm the bride-to-be, we are taking *you* to get a manicure tomorrow."

Maddie crossed her arms, tucking her offending fingers under her arms. Her hands could use some attention. Her entire life could use a makeover right about now.

She explained what had happened—how she and Zach had had a deal that they would work together.

Yet, he had not only cut her out, he'd completely kept her in the dark.

"So, let me get this straight," Val said. "He went behind your back and met with Madison? Without you?"

Maddie nodded. At least someone understood why she was so upset.

"Did he have a good reason?"

"He said it was a *personal* lunch," Maddie said. "He was meeting a *friend.*"

Zach McCarter was great at playing the *friend* card.

"He said he wanted to ease into talking about the deal. But we all know that if Dave Madison has a meeting with Zach and me on the books for Monday he's going to ask him what it's about. I know they discussed business. Now I can't trust him to have told me everything. Maybe he's keeping an ace up his sleeve for Dad."

Val squinted at her as if she wasn't completely siding with Maddie.

"What?" Maddie said as Schuyler sat down beside her with a nail file and a small bottle. She extracted Maddie's left hand and began rubbing oil on her cuticles.

"I know you might not like this," Val said tentatively. "But would you have been comfortable attending that lunch?"

Yes, because if Zach had invited me, it might have meant that he wanted me to be part of his life outside of the office. First, the kiss, next, lunch with his friend... who also happened to hold the key to a promotion for one of us.

Maddie shrugged. "I don't know what I think anymore. All I know is I've always believed that nice guys finish last and somewhere along the way, I've gotten soft. But no more."

"Maybe you just need to view this as an opportunity that will set you one step closer to clinching the deal," Val said.

"I mean, the guy does have a personal life outside the office, right?" Schuyler said.

There was a certain look in Val's eyes and while Schuyler was engrossed with salvaging Maddie's nails, Maddie did her best to silently telegraph a message to Val: *Do not, under any circumstances, reveal what you saw last night at the Thirsty Ox.*

"Zach was so sneaky about it," Maddie said. "Now I don't know if I can trust him to be fair about everything."

"Business is never fair, Mads," Val said. "You taught me that. Now, love is a different story. You have to trust the man you love one-hundred percent."

Schuyler's head popped up. She had a gleam in her eyes. "And are we talking business or love here? That makes all the difference in the world."

"We are talking business," Maddie said. "One hundred percent business and only business."

Val eyed her skeptically.

"That's the unsettling part," Maddie said before Val could out her. "My life is one hundred percent business. And then Dad yanked the rug out from under me..."

Maddie's eyes began to well up with tears. Geez, what was wrong with her? When had she gone so soft?

All it took was one "Oh, honey" and a hug from

Schuyler before the full-blown waterworks started flowing.

"I have sacrificed everything for Fortunado Real Estate," Maddie said, as she let the tears roll down her cheeks. "I haven't dated. I haven't had fun outside of Friday happy hour at the Thirsty Ox. I've put my life on hold and now I'm twenty-nine years old and what do I have? What if all that sacrifice has been for nothing? What if I never have what you have with Carlo, Sky?"

The emptiness inside her felt cavernous. She was tempted to fill it with the rest of the cookies and cupcakes, which her sisters had moved to the living room coffee table after Zach had gone. She glanced at the plate and contemplated doing a face-plant in the cupcakes and drowning her sorrows. But then she'd just hate herself for losing what little control she had left.

She swiped at a tear and sucked in a deep breath.

She couldn't tell if her sisters' silence made it better or worse. At least they were giving her time to get a grip on herself.

She so needed to get over Zach McCarter. Any lingering feelings should have died the minute her father had announced his plans. Despite tonight's throwback feel, she wasn't in high school. She was a grown woman who needed to remember that the object of her desire—the *former* object of her desire—was now the person who stood between her and her life's plan.

As Schuyler resumed conditioning Maddie's cuticles, Val started the movie *13 Going on 30*. As her sisters lost themselves in the movie, Maddie allowed herself to remember her kiss with Zach one last time.

What a dreadfully bad idea that had been.

She wasn't anything like the women he dated. The women she'd seen Zach with were pretty—stunning, even. Trophy wife material.

Ugh. How boring an existence would that be?

Your one job was to look gorgeous and never, ever grow old. Or fat. That meant hours spent in hair salons. And forsaking Moonbeam Bakery cupcakes.

That would never happen.

Even if she had to be a little curvier than what might be considered socially acceptable. She wasn't fat, but she loved her sweets.

She and Moonbeam had a pledge: 'til death do we part.

Schuyler's Barbie and Ken comment sprang to mind.

With her free hand, Maddie reached up and rubbed the ends of her hair between her thumb and index finger.

If she'd been Zach's girlfriend or even girlfriend material, he would've brought her to that lunch with Dave Madison. But she wasn't his girlfriend.

Was Dave Madison cut from the same cloth? If Maddie somehow transformed into a stunner, would she be able to regain the lead that she felt had slipped away in one afternoon?

She was starting to realize that even if she had been working hard all these years, maybe she needed to do more. Obviously, she needed to do more.

Her appearance, for example. What would happen if she made just a little more effort in that area? Not the amount of time a professional trophy wife spent, of course. Who had time for that? But what if she did *more*? Got those highlights Schuyler had been talking about? They were coming into summer. She could ask the hairdresser to make it subtle. Subtle and professional. As much as she loved being outside, they'd probably fade naturally.

Her sisters laughed at a part in the movie as Maddie scrolled through her phone checking her email.

An e-newsletter from Robinson Computers caught her eye.

She opened it.

Carlo's cousin Alejandro Mendoza was married to Olivia Fortune Robinson, one of the heiresses of Robinson Computers. Carlo had introduced Maddie to the couple and she had sold them a house.

Based on something their grandmother had said to Schuyler before she passed away, Schuyler had a theory that their dad, Kenneth, and Olivia's father, Gerald Robinson aka Jerome Fortune, were half brothers, which would make Olivia their half cousin. Kenneth hadn't been very keen on Schuyler pursuing her hunch. Plus, at the time, Maddie had been more concerned with matching Olivia and Alejandro with their perfect house and making a sale. At best, it would've been unprofessional to ask a client if their grandfather had had an affair with her grandmother, making them related. So, Maddie hadn't even been tempted to go down that path. Regardless of the intrigue, Maddie found Olivia, who was just as business savvy as she was beautiful, to be a fascinating woman.

She'd read business and lifestyle profiles on her. If Maddie hadn't had such a blinding case of tunnel vision, she might have noticed then that Olivia was a woman who had it all.

She was the perfect combination of trophy wife beautiful (though she was by no means a helpless damsel) and whip smart. She was beautiful but men still took her seriously.

Suddenly, realization dawned and opened her eyes to a whole world of possibility.

Maddie sat up straight. Why hadn't she thought of this before?

"Hey, guys," Maddie said. "Can I ask you a question?"

"Sure," Schuyler said without taking her eyes off the screen.

Val paused the movie and Schuyler blinked as if coming out of a trance.

"I need you to be completely honest with me."

They nodded and Maddie braced herself for brutal honesty. "Do you think the way I look is keeping me from succeeding in business? I mean, do I need a makeover?"

Maddie could hear virtual crickets during the silence as her sisters looked at each other, no doubt daring each other to speak first.

"Well, I guess your silence speaks volumes," Maddie said. "I asked you to be honest. You're not going to hurt my feelings if you say I do. Because here's what I'm thinking. Zach already has Dave Madison on his side. I need to pull out all the stops if I'm going to win the promotion. That includes making myself the very best I can be—in all areas.

"I've always put so much energy into my work performance, believing that hard work was all that matters. But look at me. I've never put much effort into my appearance. Sure, I dress for business—smart, tailored separates that allow me to present a pulled-together, no-nonsense image. But I've never bothered with makeup. Actually, I've never had the patience to learn how to use it, and I guess I never wanted to attract the type of men who valued a woman for her looks. And more important, men don't have to change their appearance to be taken seriously in business." Before she went on a tangent about gender inequality, she brought herself back to the topic.

"Look at me. I'm boring. I'm like a blank canvas that no one notices. But Zach… Last evening he came into the office all decked out in a rancher getup."

"What?" Schuyler asked. "What do you mean?"

Val shook her head, looking disappointed. "How did I miss that?"

"He had a lead that a rancher down in Sisterdale was looking to list his property. Not only did he buy Wranglers and cowboy boots, he rented a Ford F-150."

"Wranglers?" Schuyler mused. "God, I'll bet he looked hot."

He did.

"You see?" Maddie said. "He changed his appearance and you start objectifying him."

Schuyler and Val squinted at her, looking like they weren't quite buying what she was trying to sell.

"Okay, maybe that's not quite the same thing, but—"

"Did he get the listing?" Val asked.

Maddie grumbled under her breath. "Yes, but that's beside the point."

"No, it's not," said Val. "Not at all. Think about it. He wanted the listing. He did what he needed to do to get it—"

"And now he can worry about being objectified all the way to the bank," Schuyler added, looking pleased with herself.

Val laughed. "Well, something like that. What I'm trying to say is just because you put on a little lipstick, it doesn't mean you lose your integrity. You can change the words to the Eleanor Roosevelt quote to say, *the only person who can make you feel objectified is you.*"

Obviously, Val wasn't just the baby of the family. Right now, she seemed like the wisest of all her siblings. Her little sister was right.

Maddie had never been insecure. In fact, before her father's big shake-up that had her doubting everything, she would've considered herself the most confident of the siblings—or at least the most confident of her sisters. How was it that she was a mess contemplating mascara and blush?

"So, I think I need a makeover," she finally said.

Schuyler nearly fell over herself getting off the couch. "I'm going to get my makeup bag. Don't move."

"Sky, no," Maddie protested. "Come back and watch the rest of the movie."

"No, how many times have we seen that movie?" she said. "And I'm sure we'll end up watching it dozens of times in the future. But catching my big sister in the mood to let me put makeup on her face may be a once-in-a-lifetime opportunity. I need to strike while the iron is hot."

"We can do it tomorrow," Maddie said. "I'm really not in the mood to do it tonight. Besides, this weekend is supposed to be about you. And it feels like all the attention has been focused on me. I'm really sorry about that."

"Nonsense," said Sky. "This weekend is already turning into exactly the kind of weekend I wanted—time with my sisters. Now, it's my party and I say we're going to give you a makeover. So, sit tight. I'll be right back."

Since Maddie needed to stop by the office the next morning, she opted to go home for the night. She and her sisters were going to brunch Sunday morning, but Maddie decided it would be a good idea to sleep at her own house so that she could shower, change clothes and get an early start. Truth be told, she could probably shower, dress and get in and out of the office before her sisters were even ready to go.

On her way home that night, wearing the makeover that Schuyler had given her, she wondered if she should stop by the twenty-four-hour drugstore and pick up the things that her sister had used on her.

Maddie had to admit the makeup felt surprisingly good on her face and looked more natural than she'd thought possible. She'd envisioned makeup to feel heavy and irritating, like a mask or an unnatural coating of wax that would smudge and drip as she got hot and irritable under its weight.

Not so.

Maddie couldn't even feel it.

She looked like herself. Only better. More polished and pulled together than she'd ever looked in her entire life.

Who knew?

When Maddie had expressed her surprise and joy, her sisters had carefully made all the right noises, telling her she was beautiful just the way she was—only with a little help she was knockdown, drop-dead gorgeous.

"Do you know who you look like?" Schuyler had asked. "Val, who does she look like? You must see it. OMG, tell me you see it. She looks like Blake Lively. Do you know how long I've wanted to put just a little bit of makeup on your face? Not that you're not perfectly fine without it. But who wants to be perfectly fine when you can be gorgeous? Isn't she gorgeous, Val?"

In her exuberance, Schuyler hadn't even given Val a chance to get a word in.

"She looks just like Blake Lively. Wow! I can't believe I never noticed your potential."

Maddie chuckled at the memory as she drove home. At a stoplight, she adjusted the rearview mirror so she could glance at herself. It wasn't out of vanity as much as it was disbelief and…happiness.

What would Zach do if he could see me now? Would he be eager to take me to lunch with a guy like Dave Madison?

The neon sign of a twenty-four-hour drugstore caught Maddie's eye. She glanced at the clock on her dashboard. It was after midnight, but impulse had her flipping on her turn signal and steering her car into the parking lot.

Schuyler had insisted that after brunch they were going to go shopping for cosmetics for Maddie. She was going to get a professional beauty advisor at one of the high-end department stores to recreate the look for her and teach her about good skin care.

"You'll need to remove your makeup every night and start with a nice fresh, moisturized face every morning," Schuyler had said. "You need a lot of product. Oh, you are going to make some lucky beauty advisor very happy tomorrow. It's going to be a great sale, because you need everything."

No. Not everything. Baby steps, Sky. Baby steps.

She would remove her makeup every night because she didn't want to ruin her skin, but she'd keep the mild cleansing bar her dermatologist had recommended. She didn't have time for a complicated beauty regime that called for dozens of little jars, tubes and bottles and made her bathroom counter look like her own personal cosmetics department.

Plus, with the way Schuyler was talking, it sounded like it would take hours to get everything redone. Tomorrow would be about Schuyler. Not about Maddie.

As she entered the drugstore, she picked up a shopping basket to hold her treasures. On her way to the cosmetics aisle, she recalled the steps that Schuyler had painstakingly explained.

Pheew, she thought as she surveyed the options that took up the entire length of mirrored wall and the shelves behind her. She believed in choice, but this was overwhelming.

What was the brand that Schuyler had used?

She looked around to see if she could spot a store clerk to help her, but remembered it was midnight. She was lucky the place was open. A couple of rows behind her a gaggle of girls who looked barely old enough to be out this late, much less old enough to buy wine, were giggling over the labels.

Nope. If she was going to do this, she was in this alone.

Come on. It can't be that hard. You can do this. Just pick out some things and go home.

She picked up a bottle of foundation that claimed it created a dewy glow.

She matched a bottle to her inner arm. It was the lightest shade. That reinforced that she really needed to get out of the office and get some color. But this would have to do for now because she didn't want an orangey ridge at the base of her jawline. She wanted to look natural.

Like herself, only better.

In addition to foundation, she chose a plum-brown eye shadow—because Schuyler said a slightly purplish brown would bring out the blue of her eyes. She put a black eyeliner pencil in her basket, along with black mascara—very simple.

See, this wasn't so hard.

She decided that she wouldn't mind a bolder color lipstick. She perused the different shades—every color under the rainbow. Literally.

Who wore blue lipstick?

She recalled the girl who worked the counter at the dry cleaner where Maddie took her clothes. Her lipstick had been an iridescent navy. In a strange, individualistic way, the girl wore it well. Obviously, that's what makeup was about—discovering your comfort level and wearing the product with confidence.

She needed a lipstick that conveyed she was a strong, powerful businesswoman.

Red.

Red was a power color.

They didn't have testers. She had to trust the color swatches on the end of the tubes. She chose one called Million Dollar Red.

Blush. She chose a package of powder blusher she thought was the right shade.

Schuyler had started to teach her how to use dark and shimmery light powders to contour her face—to give the illusion of sharper cheekbones and a smaller nose—but Maddie had called it quits.

"Let me learn the basic techniques before you try to turn me into a master sculptor," she had insisted.

Remarkably, Schuyler had agreed.

By the time she brought home her treasures, Maddie was too keyed up to sleep. She took one last lingering look at the way Schuyler had done her makeup. She even snapped a couple of selfies with her smartphone and then she washed her face.

She had to get up early to get in and out of the office in time to meet Val and Schuyler for brunch. So, she put on her pajamas and went to bed even though she wasn't the least bit tired.

She did her breathing exercises, inhaling for four counts, holding the breath for seven counts, and exhaling for eight counts. Even after ten rounds, she couldn't quiet her noisy mind.

Thoughts kept jumping from kissing Zach, to arguing with Zach, to whether she would run into Zach at the office so they could smooth things out before their meeting on Monday morning. If Dave Madison sensed that there was tension in the air, it might compromise the deal. Dave would need to be sure that Zach and Maddie could work together, and while Maddie still didn't appreciate Zach not being completely up front with her, she needed to get past it. She needed to turn it around to her advantage.

She sat up in bed and turned on the lamp on the bedside table. Looking slightly annoyed, Ramona opened one sleepy eye but didn't move from her pillow bed on the floor next to Maddie's bed. There was no sense lying there stewing over it.

"Sorry, girl. Go back to sleep. At least someone is getting some rest tonight."

Maddie swung her legs over the side of the bed and padded over to the en suite bath. Her cosmetics were lying on the built-in vanity counter still in the bag. She sat down at the vanity, opened the packages and lined them up till they looked like soldiers at the ready. Soldiers that would help her win this battle.

She opened the bottle of foundation and poured a dab

out onto the back of her hand, as she'd seen Schuyler do, and began applying the opaque liquid to her face.

She'd purposely opted to go a little lighter to look more natural—but had she gone too light?

It didn't look like what Sky had put on her.

It was late, but Maddie was wide-awake and eager to try on the rest so that she'd know what she was facing in the morning before she went into the office. Because, of course, if Zach was in the office, she'd want him to see the new her while she pretended that she was still the old her.

She picked up the brown eye shadow next. In contrast to the base makeup, it looked much darker than it had appeared in the packaging.

After poking herself in the eye with the mascara wand, which made her eyes water—and water—and water—and getting overzealous with the red lipstick, she couldn't decide if she looked more like a scary clown or Heath Ledger's Joker.

Oh, this was bad.

Obviously, it was *that* hard to make makeup look effortless and natural.

As she scrubbed her face clean, she decided that maybe she needed more practice before she debuted her new look.

She towel dried her face then rubbed her index finger over her red-tinged lips. The lipstick had feathered beyond the boundaries, forming a ring around her mouth that looked as if she'd been eating a cherry snow cone. She hoped she hadn't permanently stained them. It was almost 2:00 a.m. At this rate, she'd do well to get five hours' sleep if she got up in time to make it to the office and back to meet her sisters.

She climbed back into bed and drifted asleep dreaming up a plan that would allow her to make things right with Zach and win the promotion.

Chapter Seven

Zach had a potential buyer for the Winters ranch in Sisterdale. He'd let Jim and Mary Ann know that he was bringing Joanna and Gary Everly by around eleven thirty. He'd rented the truck again. It comfortably seated six, so the three of them would have plenty of room for the long trip.

The Everlys were meeting him at the office at seven thirty Sunday morning. He'd stopped by the bakery and picked up a dozen donuts and three cups of coffee for the trip. He was fifteen minutes early, which gave him just enough time to go inside and grab the spec sheet for the property. When he pulled into the parking lot and saw Maddie's white Volvo, his stomach tightened—and not in an altogether bad way.

She'd been right last night—or at least partially

right—when she'd said he hadn't been up front with her about meeting Dave Madison for lunch. He should've told her before he went. He was glad to have this opportunity to clear the air before seeing her tomorrow.

He let himself in the office and announced himself so as not to scare her, since she probably wasn't expecting anyone this early in the morning.

"Maddie?" he called from the hallway. He could hear the clicking sound of someone working on a computer keyboard. The *click-click-clickity-click* stopped the moment he'd spoken, but she didn't say anything.

"Hey," he said when he appeared in her office doorway. "I just wanted to let you know I was here. I'm meeting some clients. So, I'll be leaving in a few minutes."

"Are you showing the property down in Sisterdale?" she asked, eyeing him up and down.

"How did you know?" he asked.

"The cowboy costume."

"Yeah. My Sisterdale uniform. I'm driving some potential buyers out there today."

Maddie's gaze made a slow perusal of his body starting from his head, working its way down to his boots and back up again. When their gazes finally met, there was a hungry look in her eyes.

"Well, now that you've undressed me with your eyes…" he said.

"Zach," she said. "Don't."

"Don't do what, Maddie?"

The pink of her cheeks deepened. Her lips looked particularly alluring this morning. He wondered how he'd never noticed before, never *seen* her before. But now he couldn't unsee her and he didn't want to.

That kiss had awakened something in him—an undeniable attraction, a dormant hunger. And he was dying for another taste. He was dying for her. He wanted to pull her close and strip away every barrier between them.

"I should have told you about my meeting with Dave Madison before I went. I don't know why I didn't, other than I'm not used to considering others when I work. I've always flown solo—in work and in my personal life. Which brings me to the real point. I don't think my lunch with Dave Madison is the problem here."

"Of course it is," she snapped a little too fast. "I mean, but not anymore. I appreciate you seeing my point of view. So, we're good."

She waved him away and turned her body squarely toward her computer and started typing. She was focusing a little too hard on the screen. She seemed to be taking great pains not to look at him.

"Are we okay, Maddie?"

"Sure. Your client will probably be here any minute now, and I have to get my work done. I'm meeting Schuyler and Val for brunch. We need to salvage what's left of her bachelorette weekend."

He leaned his hip on her desk, intending to show her he wasn't in a hurry to leave her. "You do realize Val called me and invited me over last night, right? I didn't just show up."

She frowned at him. "Of course."

"Then, if my lunch with Dave Madison and my

crashing your party last night aren't the problems, I can think of only one other thing that could be bothering you."

She pushed her chair away from her desk with a swift shove and leaned toward him. "Why would you think something is bothering me, Zach?"

"First of all, your tone."

She crossed her arms. "Sorry. My mom used to say, 'You don't hear you the way others hear you.'" Something in her demeanor softened. "I don't mean to sound bitchy. I'm really not a bitch, Zach."

"I know you're not."

She gave a one-shoulder shrug. "Wouldn't qualities that come across as bitchy be applauded if I were a man? Or maybe not applauded. They wouldn't even be noticed."

Their gazes fused for a combustible instant.

He noticed her. He wanted to tell her he noticed her, that he couldn't take his eyes off her, but the faint sound of someone knocking on the front door broke the spell and pulled him back into the here and now.

"That's my clients," he said. "They're early."

"You better not keep them waiting, then."

Maddie scooted her chair back to her desk and glanced at her computer monitor again, the color still high on her pretty cheeks.

What almost happened there? If Joanna and Gary Everly hadn't arrived early he would've leaned in and kissed her. He'd wanted to kiss her. But he hadn't been as fearless as she'd been that night at the Thirsty Ox. Now they were out of time.

"For the record, I don't think you're bitchy," he said. "I think you're passionate. Don't ever apologize for, or feel bad about, being passionate."

He thought she was passionate.

Passionate.

It might've been the nicest compliment anyone had ever paid her.

"Earth to Maddie?" Schuyler said. "Armand wants to know if you'd like another bloody Mary?"

Maddie realized her sisters and the very handsome waiter, who had been flirting with them since the moment he'd introduced himself, were staring at her.

Maddie glanced down, unsure whether her glass was full or empty or somewhere in between, saw that there was only a splash at the bottom.

"Yes, please. That would be lovely."

"You're in a good mood today," Val said. "A little dreamy, but I don't know when I've seen you so relaxed."

Maddie smiled and shrugged. "Really? Why wouldn't I be happy when I get the chance to hang out with my sisters?"

Schuyler and Val exchanged dubious looks.

"Since you went home last night," Schuyler said, "I was afraid you were mad at me for asking Zach to come over last night."

Maddie feigned confusion. "Why would I be mad?" She hadn't been happy about it. But if her sisters hadn't meddled and she and Zach hadn't argued, they wouldn't have made up this morning. If not for them, she might never have known that he thought she was *passionate*.

"Even if I was upset—which I'm not, I promise— I wouldn't spoil the last day of our girls' weekend by pouting. And speaking of, after we try on our bridesmaid dresses, what would you like to do this afternoon, Sky? We could go wander around the Japanese Gardens, or I hear that they just opened a brand-new exhibit of the French Impressionist painters at the Museum of Fine Arts. Or there's that new movie with Zoe Kazan that looks great."

"All of those options sound great." Schuyler sipped the fresh bloody Mary the waiter had stealthily set in front of her. "I think we'd just better stick with shopping today. I wish we had more time, but I still have some things to pull together for the wedding. Can you believe Carlo and I will be married in less than a week?" Schuyler wrung her hands.

"Are you nervous?" Val asked.

A wistful smile overtook Schuyler's face. "Not really nervous as much as I'm excited. I just want everything to be perfect. I keep thinking of little things I've forgotten."

"You know nothing is perfect," said Maddie. "But the imperfections will give you fabulous stories to tell later. You've hired the best wedding planner in Texas. She'll handle those little things and she'll have your back. So, you should use this last week of singlehood to relax."

"She's not going to make sure I have the perfect thing to wear on my wedding night," Schuyler said. "I need to find something. I can't believe I almost forgot."

"But what about all the gorgeous things you got at your lingerie shower?" Val asked.

"I know," Schuyler said. "Every single thing was gorgeous, but I have something specific in mind. Do you all mind if we go to the Galleria after the dress fittings so I can look?"

"The bride's wish is our command," said Maddie.

"You are sneaky." Maddie slanted a glance at Schuyler, who smiled a victorious smile.

Schuyler hadn't wanted to come to the Galleria to find a perfect piece of lingerie to wear on her wedding night. It had been an ambush to get Maddie into the cosmetics department and into the chair she now sat in for a professional makeover.

If she'd poked herself in the eye three times last night applying a simple coat of mascara, how on earth was she going to replicate the fine line that Cheryl, the makeup artist, had just drawn on her right eyelid? And Maddie had to attempt it with one eye closed? It made her hands shake contemplating the idea. If she created a distraction, could she make a getaway?

"Here," Cheryl said, handing Maddie the slim brush. "You do the other eye. You'll see how easily it glides on."

Maddie waved her off. "You've done such a nice job with my makeup, I don't want to ruin it."

"But you see, that's just it," Cheryl said. "Try it, you'll see that it's virtually foolproof."

Foolproof? Hahaha!

Maddie was tempted to counter with her scary clown

tale from the night before, but suddenly, arguing her point felt more exhausting than just trying. She accepted the brush, leaned in to the mirror and followed Cheryl's instructions.

To Maddie's amazement and utter delight, the liner went on as magically as Cheryl had promised. And then, so did the mascara and lipstick.

As Cheryl stepped back and surveyed the results, Schuyler and Val voiced their approval.

The woman handed Maddie a hand mirror. "Simple, fresh and natural. Best of all, this look is fast and easy to do."

If Schuyler's impromptu makeover had been good, this one was nothing short of astounding.

"She'll take everything," Schuyler said with a sweep of her hand as if reading her mind.

Cheryl smiled at Maddie. "I promise this look will take you less than seven minutes in the morning. Just think, a whole new gorgeous you in less time than it takes to brew a cup of coffee."

A whole new me. That's something.

What was important was how much Schuyler seemed to be reveling in the idea that Maddie was amenable to not only wearing makeup at her wedding, but learning how to make it a part of her daily routine. She got the distinct feeling that even though her sister was too kind to come right out and say it, Maddie's professional makeover may have been one of the missing parts that Schuyler had been fretting over during brunch.

Maddie felt a little selfish pretending she was doing this all for Schuyler. Sure, she was a big part of the reason, but an anxious giddiness was forming in the pit of her stomach as she contemplated seeing Zach tomorrow morning.

What would Zach think of a more polished, passionate Maddie?

"While we're at it," Schuyler said when Cheryl went to package her purchases, "let's talk about your wardrobe."

"My wardrobe is just fine," Maddie said. "It's all from Brooks Brothers. I love that brand. It's one-stop shopping. Quick and efficient. Angie has been my specialist since I got back to Houston after college. She calls me once a year and reminds me it's time to come in. She lays out an assortment of classic pieces I can mix and match and has them ready for me to try on. She shows me how I can get two weeks' worth of outfits out of five or so pieces."

Schuyler and Val looked amused, but not at all impressed.

"Yes, we're familiar with your style, Mads," said Val.

Her sisters exchanged a look.

"Boring," Schuyler sang under her breath.

"You really should think about working some color and pattern into your neutrals," Val said.

"Or scrapping the neutrals altogether and getting a new wardrobe with some pizzazz," Schuyler said.

Uh-oh. Had she created a monster by letting Schuyler herd her into the makeover chair?

"Hey, my neutrals are fine," Maddie said. "And I do pair them with colorful blouses every once in a while. And what about my teal dress? That's colorful. My wardrobe is easy. One less thing to worry about in the morning, especially now that I'll have to dedicate time to makeup."

"Seven minutes, Mads," Schuyler said. "Seven minutes will hardly derail your schedule." She waved her hand, as if shooing away Maddie's argument. "I know of a shop that helps disadvantaged women get back into the workplace that would love to have your neutrals. You'll be getting new clothes to go with your new look. Believe me, after I get through with you, you're going to thank me when you see yourself. But first, after we finish here, we're going to get your hair cut—"

"No!" Maddie insisted, as she paid for her cosmetics. "That's where I draw the line. You are not touching my hair."

It turned out that Schuyler didn't lay a hand on Maddie's hair, but Jade, the stylist Sky still traveled from Austin to Houston to see every six weeks, ended up having her way with Maddie's locks.

It was a mystery how Jade managed to be available at the exact moment that the Fortunado sisters arrived, since Sky often bemoaned how she had to book her appointments months out.

Maddie was beginning to sense a conspiracy, but she had to admit it was fun seeing herself transform right before her own eyes. It was a learning experience and a reminder that sometimes the old way of doing things needed a little sprucing up.

Jade listened to Maddie's concern for needing low-maintenance hair.

"I don't play well with round brushes and blow-dryers," Maddie told her. "If I tried to use one of those brushes, I'd probably get it stuck in my hair and have to cut it out. I don't have the time or the inclination to learn. So, let's not do anything that requires styling."

Jade assured her she would give her a style even better and more low maintenance than her current do.

First, she gave Maddie some strategically placed highlights to frame her face and give her hair some dimension. After Jade washed out the bleach, she trimmed off about three inches and cut in long layers, which Jade promised would give Maddie's thick hair more bounce. And, yes, she would still be able to pull it back into her signature ponytail.

"Just look at you," Jade exclaimed, after all was said and done. "You're stunning. I mean, you are knock-down, drop-dead gorgeous, girl. Why on earth would you want to hide these tresses in a pony? That's a sin."

For the first time ever, Maddie wondered the same thing. Her hair felt lighter and bouncier. When she ran her fingers through it, it was silky to the touch and fell neatly back into place. Suddenly, it seemed a heck of a lot more professional than a ponytail.

Val stayed behind to have Jade work her magic on her hair, while Schuyler dragged Maddie to Hattie's Boutique for a look at her spring collection.

Even though Schuyler had been living in Austin for the past several months, she still knew all the best places to shop in Houston. Schuyler seemed to be having so much fun with their shopping adventure that Maddie embraced the possibility that they would be visiting each and every one of her sister's favorite shops. For the first time in her life, she was enjoying shopping.

The funky, fashion-forward boutiques were a far cry from Brooks Brothers' professional offerings.

It was like taking a trip to a foreign country. It wasn't necessarily her lifestyle, but she could embrace it for an afternoon. When in Rome...or when in boho boutiques... do as your sisters do. She'd never minded investing in classic pieces that would outlast trends and time, but some of the trendiest pieces Schuyler and the shopgirls picked out for her cost three times her normal purchases.

These clothes were expensive and attention-grabbing.

Unlike her glamorous, sassy sister, who had been more like their late grandmother—whom they'd all called Glammy after a childhood speech impediment caused Schuyler to mispronounce *Grammy*—Maddie wanted to wear the clothes. She didn't want loud colors and screaming patterns to wear her.

Such as the red, orange and yellow Emilio Pucci shift dress Schuyler was handing Maddie over the louvered dressing room door.

"Oh, no," Maddie said. "Not this one." She opened the door a crack and peeked out. Schuyler was wearing a black-and-florescent-pink maxi dress that played tricks on Maddie's vision. The dress suited her sister. But this Pucci number... "It's too bright. If I wore this, someone would mistake me for a stolen Picasso painting."

"That's right," Schuyler said. "With your body and legs, you'll look definitely like a work of art in this dress. Put it on and come out so I can see you in it."

Schuyler let go of the clothes hanger. Rather than

letting the crazy dress fall to the floor, Maddie caught it and closed the fitting room door. She eyed the getup. It wasn't her at all. She held the dress up to her body and looked in the mirror to prove that point—that it was exactly the opposite of everything she stood for. It was loud and obnoxiously bright. It was attention-seeking and...*fun*.

With her new makeup and freer, lighter, looser hair, it looked fun.

She couldn't help but try to imagine Zach's face if she showed up to their meeting tomorrow morning wearing a dress like this.

No. I couldn't. I'd feel too conspicuous. It's so not me.

That's when a little voice in her head said, *If you keep doing what you're doing, you'll keep getting what you're getting.* Like not having her body of work be good enough to win a promotion on its own. Or like having to kiss a guy first and have him seem like he was interested, but hang back enough to make her wonder if he was interested or if it was just flirty business as usual.

Or even worse, if he'd upped the flirting ante simply to throw her off her game.

But he'd called her *passionate*. She was passionate about her job. About Zach. He'd recognized the fire in her, even when she hadn't seen it herself—or at least known what to call it.

She'd called it bitchy. He'd called it passionate.

A passionate woman shouldn't be afraid to take a risk. At least not with something as low-risk as clothes.

She slipped the dress over her head, loving the expensive feel of the silky fabric as it glided down her body. She fluffed her hair, which fell back into place perfectly, and adjusted the dress so that it sat right on her.

Oh, no.

It was too short and so bright it bordered on vulgar. Sort of. It did call attention to itself. To her.

"Do you have it on?" Schuyler called.

But it also skimmed her curves as if Pucci had made it just for her. It hit her about three inches above the knees, which automatically made it inappropriate for the office, but… If she looked at it through another lens, a different lens, it was a playful romp of a dress that might be fun to wear after hours.

As if she ever went out. Other than Fridays at the Thirsty Ox, her after hours were spent at home with Ramona. Her little dog loved her just the way she was. In fact, the garish pattern might scare her.

And that was one of the dumbest lies she'd ever told herself.

A knock sounded on the dressing room door. "Open up, Mads. I want to see the dress on you."

Feeling overwhelmingly shy and completely out of her element, Maddie opened the dressing room door a crack. Schuyler took it from there and yanked it the rest of the way open.

"Oh, my gosh, look at you!" Schuyler *squeed.* Maddie had heard the word *squee* used before—usually in a text from one of her sisters, but until that moment, she'd never actually heard the sound. The noise Schuyler was making was most definitely a *squee*.

"You look absolutely gorge." Schuyler clapped her hands and bounced a little in her enthusiasm. "Turn around."

Schuyler made a circular motion with her index finger and Maddie complied, feeling strangely giddy at her sister's reaction.

"You have to get this dress, Mads. We are not leaving here without it."

"I don't know, Sky."

Schuyler grabbed Maddie's hand and pulled her over to a set of three-way mirrors at the end of the rectangular dressing room.

"Look at you. Just look at you."

Schuyler clasped her hands together and held them under her chin in a way that reminded Maddie so much of Glammy it almost took her breath away. Glammy, who'd been their father's mother, hadn't even been gone a year, but of all the siblings, Schuyler had inherited her tendency toward the overly dramatic, just like Glammy.

Before their grandmother died, she had set Schuyler on a mission to prove that the Fortunado crew was related to the infamous Fortunes, a vast, wealthy family who, due to Jerome Fortune's affairs, had ever-expanding branches in the southeast and England. But their father had put a hard stop to Schuyler's digging, saying he was proud of his background and who he'd become without any help from the Fortunes. He was a self-made man who had parlayed a lottery win into a real estate empire. Glammy, whose name had been Mary before she'd changed it to Starlight, had single-handedly raised him without help from her only son's father. Anytime anyone questioned Kenneth Fortunado about his father, he claimed he didn't know who his dad was and didn't care. Since Glammy's passing, speculation was that Julius Fortune, Jerome's father, was his biological father, but Kenneth maintained he didn't care if that was the truth. He had his six kids and his wife—and he certainly had enough money that he didn't need any Fortune money. He had instructed everyone to leave well enough alone.

"Maddie?" Schuyler said. "Are you okay?"

Maddie shook her head. "Yeah, sure. For a moment there you reminded me so much of Glammy it knocked the breath out of me."

"Oh." Schuyler drew in an audible breath that hitched and her eyes welled. Maddie was afraid that her sister might start crying. All of her siblings had loved Glammy, but Schuyler was the closest to her. Like two peas in a pod. Schuyler had said the only reason her wedding wouldn't be perfect was because Glammy wouldn't be here to see it.

To help her sister regain her composure, Maddie said, "Would this dress be appropriate for work?"

She knew it wasn't, but the bulldog had dropped her bone and Maddie was delivering it to her so she could get a better grip.

Schuyler drew in another shaky breath, but this time she focused her gaze on the dress.

"No, not for work. But it would be perfect for the rehearsal dinner. Come with me. There's an adorable hot pink Kate Spade fit and flare out here I want you to see.

It has a jewel neckline and it's sleeveless so it will be perfect for this summer when the weather turns warm."

Schuyler found her sister's size and sent her toward the fitting room. The pink dress was cute—for Schuyler. But it was such a departure from what Maddie was used to. Even so, she tried it on.

With the help of the sales associate, Schuyler pulled several more dresses that she deemed fun, fashionable and work-appropriate for Maddie. She also pulled a pair of strappy gold sandals. Her sister might have been wasting her calling working as special events coordinator for the Mendoza Winery. With her affinity and flare for fashion, she should have her own boutique.

The Kate Spade fit like a dream and Maddie had to admit that the vibrant shades and geometric patterns of the other selections were pretty. Actually, they were downright exquisite, but she didn't feel 100 percent natural when she tried them on. But the pink dress felt as if it were made for her.

"You look great," Schuyler insisted. "Do you think I would steer you wrong?"

"Not on purpose."

"Oh, please." Her sister rolled her eyes. "Get the yellow-and-orange Pucci for the rehearsal dinner and, for now, just get one new dress for work. I vote for the Kate Spade. You're going to feel so drab when you try to go back to your old boring neutrals that you'll be back to buy a whole new wardrobe. How much do you want to bet?"

Maddie frowned at herself in the three-way mirror.

"I just don't know, Sky. It's a lot of change all at once. I don't even look like myself anymore."

"You look like you, only better. It really isn't that drastic because you've always been beautiful. But just more like a blank canvas waiting for someone to come in and paint you at your very best."

They locked eyes in the mirror.

"You don't believe me?" Schuyler asked. "Go put that pink Kate Spade back on. I'll be right back. Come out into the store when you're dressed."

Maddie squinted at Schuyler. "What are you up to?"

"Just shoo." Schuyler made a sweeping gesture with her hand. "Go change and meet me by the sales desk."

By the time Maddie emerged dressed in the pink number, Schuyler had assembled a panel of six guys.

"Guys, meet my sister Maddie. Isn't she hot?"

What the hell?

As the guys murmured their agreement, Maddie shot daggers at Schuyler with her eyes. What were they supposed to say being put on the spot like that?

This was one of the most awkward moments of her life. Almost as awkward as the aftermath of kissing Zach. She wanted to duck behind the sales desk or run out the front door. She would've if she hadn't been wearing the unpaid-for dress. Instead, she turned to go change.

"Where do you think you're going?" Schuyler asked.

"Away from here."

"That's just rude," Schuyler said. "These guys want to meet you. Don't you, guys?"

Again, they murmured their agreement.

"Maddie is single, but works too much. So, she doesn't get out a lot. I want a show of hands. If you saw my sister out somewhere wearing this dress, would you ask her out? Raise your hand if you would."

To Maddie's flummoxed surprise, all six hands went up.

She felt her face flame. Judging by the intensity, it was probably the same color as her dress. If not brighter.

Bride-to-be or not, she was going to kill her sister.

"This has been very awkward," Maddie said to the guys. "Thank you for being so nice. I apologize on behalf of my sister. You all have been great sports, but you're free to go now."

One guy left, but the other five stayed. The tallest one with dark hair said, "Can I get your number?"

My number?

For the first time, Maddie allowed herself to really look at the guy. He was cute, but he looked a little young.

"What's your name?" Maddie asked.

"Drew," the guy answered.

Maddie smiled at him. "Drew, you're a sweetheart. Do you mind if I ask how old you are?"

He chuckled. "Nineteen."

"Ah, nineteen." Maddie mustered her best smile as she turned to her sister. "Drew is nineteen, Schuyler."

"So, what," Schuyler countered. "He has good taste."

"Drew, if I were five years younger I'd go out with you in a heartbeat." Okay, maybe seven years younger. But she didn't need to tell Drew that. She didn't want to hurt his feelings after he'd put himself on the line like that. "But I'm too old for you. You need someone a little more age appropriate."

"It's okay. I dig older chicks. What are you, like thirty-four?"

I'm twenty-nine and you're a child. Go back to the playground.

"Thirty-four, huh?" She shot Schuyler another scalding look. "Something like that. It was nice to meet you. It was nice to meet all of you."

She turned around and felt like she was doing the walk of shame to the dressing room, where she locked herself in and contemplated not coming out. She had a protein bar in her purse and a half-full bottle of water that Jade had given her at the salon. She could live quite comfortably in here.

She took her time changing and hanging up the dozen dresses she'd tried on. The entire time she gave herself a pep talk. Schuyler was only trying to help. She really did mean well. And the guys had been nice. They'd all raised their hands when polled about whether they'd date her. Why did this feel so humiliating? It should bolster her self-esteem.

She lowered herself onto the fabric-covered bench and sat with the feeling for a moment. Really, *humiliating* wasn't the right word. Sure, she'd been jolted out of her comfort zone. But that wasn't necessarily a bad thing. In fact, she thought as she looked at herself in the mirror, a lot of good had come from today.

Even if Drew, the one who dug older chicks, had aged her by five years, she should be flattered by his clumsy compliment. In fact, all the guys had been flattering.

So, what was wrong here?

Why was this not settling very well with her?

Because they're not Zach.

The realization made her breath hitch and the pit of her stomach tingle in a way that only happened when she thought of Zach.

"Chin up, buttercup." Schuyler's voice carried through the louvered door. "Six out of six dudes surveyed say Madeleine Fortunado is a hot tamale. But she needs to work on her game. For the record, they didn't say that. I added that part, and you know it's true. I can help you with that, too. But one step at a time."

They're not Zach.

What was she going to do?

She touched the hem of the pink Kate Spade dress and rubbed the fabric between her fingers before looking at the price tag.

Yikes. It cost more than the price of two of her usual pieces and she really couldn't mix and match it with anything. If she tried to pair it with one of her blazers, she'd look like she'd borrowed one of Zach's sports coats.

Zach.

Did he think she dressed manly? Not really manly as much as conservatively. Neutral. What was it Schuyler called it? Boring.

Maddie liked things straightforward, in fashion and in life. She liked things to match. When things didn't match up or varied from her well-ordered plans, it threw her off-kilter.

Maybe the reason Zach threw off her equilibrium—

and threw her off-kilter—the way he did was because he messed with her well-ordered system. He made her think and feel things that didn't have a place in her world.

Maybe she should buy the dresses—the pink Kate Spade and the yellow-and-orange Pucci. She'd wear the Pucci to the rehearsal dinner to make Sky happy. She'd get the gold sandals, too. And maybe she'd get the pink dress and wear that little number into the office tomorrow.

She knew she was good at what she did. No amount of makeup or pretty dresses could disprove that truth. But now she had to admit there was room for improvement. For a different approach.

Another knock sounded on the door. "Mads, are you okay in there? Don't be mad at me."

Maddie opened the door. "I'm not mad at you, Sky, but thanks for the most mortifying afternoon of my life." She turned and gave her sister a hug. "And the best afternoon of my life, too."

Schuyler hugged her back and then pulled away holding Maddie at arm's length. "Look at you. You're like a beautiful butterfly who has burst from her cocoon."

"It's a chrysalis."

"What did you say?" Schuyler asked.

"A butterfly emerges from a chrysalis, not a cocoon."

Schuyler waved her off. "Okay, whatever. You're like the duckling who has finally blossomed into the swan."

She started to explain that ducks and swans were two different birds, but she stopped herself.

"All right, Miss Simile, let's not get carried away."

Schuyler laughed. "We just have one last thing to do before my work here is done. We're going to get manis and pedis. Then you will be the complete package."

As they walked into the nail salon, Schuyler said, "Three of those dudes gave me their phone numbers and want you to call them."

"Three including Drew?"

"No, three other than Drew. He wanted to ask you out. So, technically, all six thought you were hot, and four of the six were willing to put their money where their mouth was. Are you going to call them?"

Maddie had to admit it was flattering, but... "No, I'm old-fashioned when it comes to calling guys."

But not making the first move to kiss a guy. Well, not just any guy. Zach.

"What do you mean?" Schuyler asked.

"I don't call guys. They call me."

Schuyler frowned at her. "I should have given those guys your number. Or... I could call them for you. That's what a great, loving sister I am."

"No, of course, I didn't want you to give them my number. And don't you dare call any of them. In fact, give me their numbers right now."

Maddie held out her hand but Schuyler clutched the paper tightly and held it out of Maddie's reach. "Only if you promise you'll call one of them and ask them to be your plus-one to the wedding."

Maddie's jaw fell open. "Are you crazy? I don't know those guys. Why would I invite them to an important family event? And a wedding that's out of town, for that matter."

Schuyler shrugged. "Fair enough, but who are you going to bring? I have you down as bringing a plus-one."

"There's a simple fix for that," Maddie said, as she climbed into the pedicure chair. "Take my plus-one off the list."

"Too late. I've already made the seating chart. All the names are written in gold script on a big piece of framed Plexiglas. It says Maddie Fortunado's plus-one. It can't be changed without scrapping the entire board and having it redone."

"What if someone cancels?" Maddie said over the sound of running water. The nail technicians were filling the footbaths and it was a little hard to talk over the sound.

"They'd better not cancel," Schuyler shot back. "Carlo and I kept the guest list small because we want our wedding to be intimate and elegant. Every single person who attends is someone special to us."

"Such as the six guys you dragged in off the street?" Maddie snarked. "Which one is the most special? I'd love for you to rank them in order."

Schuyler rolled her eyes, but Maddie sensed that she might have gone too far. "I gave you a plus-one because I wanted you to have a good time. Mads, I worry about you. Now that our brothers and I have moved away, and Mom and Dad are going to be traveling more, it's just you and Val."

Maddie braced herself for Schuyler to mention the fact that she had put all her eggs in one Fortunado Real

Estate basket and now that basket was proving to have some holes in it. She decided to cut her off at the pass.

"If I don't win this promotion, I'm going to leave Fortunado."

Schuyler didn't look surprised. "I can't say I blame you. Will you stay in town?"

Maddie shrugged. "I don't know. Maybe not. I haven't thought that far ahead. Dad hasn't announced his decision yet and I'm trying to stay positive."

"You're selling a lot of property in Austin lately. Why don't you move there— Oh, I almost forgot! Act surprised when he calls you, but Carlo is super interested in that last location you showed us. The one near the university. He thinks it'd make a great spot for the nightclub. He wants to make an offer before we leave for our honeymoon. But you didn't hear it from me."

"That's good news. Now I'll completely forget you said anything about it."

"So, if you win," Schuyler said, "what's Zach going to do? Because I can't imagine that Dad would really turn over the business to someone who isn't family."

"He says he's leaving if he doesn't get the promotion."

Schuyler's eyes got wide. "Like leave-leave? Leave town? Or just leave the company?"

Maddie shrugged. "He hasn't said one way or the other. But either way it would be bad. If he stays, he'd be smart to open his own office. But he'd be Fortunado's direct competition. And if he left, well…"

Maddie drew in a deep breath and closed her eyes for a moment. She hadn't wanted to think about that either.

She could see so many ways that Zach was the better man for the job. He was so connected—even only being in Houston for a few months. He just seemed to have a way of making things work. Either way, it was a lose-lose proposition. Either way she was going to lose the only man she'd been interested in in a very long time. If she hadn't loved and respected her father as much as she did, she'd be cursing him for messing up every-thing. For messing up her life.

Schuyler shook her head. "Well, that's no good. How are you two nincompoops ever going to get together if you're not even in the same town?" She let out a sigh. "I still say you two are perfect for each other."

Maddie slanted a glance at Schuyler, who had full-on relaxed into her pedi. She had cranked up the massage function on the chair, which was nearly in full recline.

She looked so happy. Maddie was thrilled for her. But it wasn't the first time that she wished she could be a little more like her free-spirited little sister. Schuyler always had faith that things would work out—and they usually did. Maddie simply couldn't act without over-thinking all the ramifications.

By the time she thought everything through, she was nearly paralyzed with indecision. So, to appear deci-sive and in control, she usually defaulted to what was comfortable.

If you keep doing what you're doing, you'll keep get-ting what you're getting.

"Sky, may I confide in you?" Maddie asked.

"You'd better." Schuyler returned her chair to the up-right position so that she was sitting as straight as the big leatherette chairs would allow. Maddie was sorry she'd disturbed her.

"Relax," Maddie said. "Put your chair back the way it was. What I have to say is really not a big deal."

Liar. It's a huge deal, if you'd only open up.

Just leap. Stop overthinking.

"This is about Zach, isn't it?"

Maddie froze, if only to keep herself from shaking her head and changing the subject.

"Don't be shy about it, about him, Maddie."

Maddie tried to say something, but she couldn't force out the words that were lodged in the back of her throat.

Schuyler cocked a brow. A cheeky expression claimed her face. "It's a good thing I love Carlo so much, because if I didn't I'd set my cap for Zach Mc-Carter."

That was all it took to dislodge the lump in Maddie's throat. She laughed so hard her eyes started to well. "Set your cap? Who are you? Jane Austen?"

Schuyler beamed at the appreciation for her joke. "I made you laugh."

"Yes, you did," Maddie said.

"That's just it," Schuyler said. "You should be laughing more, smiling more. Lately, the only time I see you laugh and smile is when you're around Zach. Otherwise you're wound tighter than Zach's ass."

"Schuyler." Maddie glanced at the nail techs who were deep in quiet conversation with each other and seemed to not be listening to them. Thank God.

"You have to admit he does have a great ass," Schuyler said. "I've noticed. No disrespect to Carlo, who has a nice ass, too. I want you to have a nice ass of your own, Mads. I mean, a guy of your own with a nice ass."

Maddie pressed her hand to her mouth to stifle her laughter. She didn't want to draw any more attention to them. "Okay. Okay. Okay. I'd love that."

"So, you're saying you've noticed Zach's great butt?"

Maddie glanced around the nail salon. It was so late in the day that there was only one other pair of women in the place and they were seated at the other end of the row of pedicure chairs not paying the least bit of attention to the sisters' conversation.

"You have, haven't you?" Schuyler wiggled her brows.

"Okay, yes. I've noticed. Who wouldn't notice?"

"Right? A person would have to be dead not to," Schuyler said. "A few minutes ago, you said you were going to confide in me about something. Dish."

Of course, Schuyler wouldn't forget a juicy offer like that. But the most important thing was that despite her sister's free-spirited ways and her tendency to make jokes about trivial matters—or to use humor to draw Maddie out of her shell—Schuyler was a great confidant. If Maddie asked her not to repeat something, Schuyler was more solid than Fort Knox.

Maddie had learned the hard way that if she didn't issue a caveat and specifically ask her not to say anything about something, all bets were off. In fact, bets would favor Schuyler repeating exactly what she'd heard—at the most inopportune time.

"So, this is just between us, okay?" Maddie said.

Schuyler leaned in and drew her thumb and forefinger over her lips, indicating that her lips were zipped.

Maddie recounted the events of Friday night at the Thirsty Ox and how she'd kissed Zach.

Actually, it felt good to throw caution to the wind and giggle about her crush with her sister. Schuyler's eyes were huge and her mouth formed a perfect O. Maddie wasn't surprised that her admission had rendered her sister momentarily speechless.

Momentarily.

"You kissed Zach?"

Maddie nodded and heat washed over her cheeks.

"And he came over Saturday night," Schuyler said.

Maddie nodded again.

"He really seemed like he was into you."

"I don't know about that."

"Well, I do. You have to ask him to the wedding, Mads."

Maddie shook her head. "No, I can't. It's not a good idea. The whole point behind the kiss was to get him out of my system."

Schuyler winced and shot Maddie an incredulous look.

"Don't judge me," Maddie said. "When you look at the facts, it only makes sense. One of us will win this promotion. The other one is leaving. Getting involved wouldn't work. That's assuming he's even interested in getting involved. Zach is a first-class flirt, Sky. So, I'm more inclined to believe that the kiss didn't mean anything to him. I kissed him because I've always had a thing for him and this way, no matter what happens, now I won't wonder what it would've been like. I guess you could say it was my consolation prize."

"No!" Schuyler shouted. Their techs looked up and the women at the other end of the row darted alarmed glances down their way.

"Sorry," Schuyler said. "Just trying to talk some sense into my sister. As you were."

The women gazed at them warily, as if they were looking at a couple of unpredictable animals.

"Schuyler, *shhhh*," Maddie admonished.

"There will be no consolation prizes here. You will not just settle for a stolen kiss. You will win the whole thing. You deserve to have everything you want."

Maddie envied her sister's Pollyanna spirit, but Maddie knew Sky was the dreamer and she was the realist.

"It is what it is," Maddie said.

"No, it is what you make it. Why is it so difficult for you to admit that there could be something between the two of you if you'd just open your heart and try? Why don't you try to figure out a way to win the promotion *and* Zach?"

Maddie's heart kicked against her rib cage.

Thump-thump, thump-thump, thump-thump.

"Why? Because I hate losing," Maddie said. "And taking a chance on Zach and missing the mark would hurt too much."

Chapter Eight

Monday morning was off to a bad start. Dave Madison had called while Zach was in the shower and left a message canceling their meeting that morning. Dave said that yesterday he'd been called away on business in Dallas and he wasn't able to make it back.

Zach wondered if the important piece of business that had detained him was blond or brunette.

Now he was left to do the dirty work: telling Maddie that Dave had canceled. Hearing the news this close to Kenneth's deadline and the fact that he'd called Zach, not Maddie, was not going to go over well. Especially since Maddie already believed Zach was trying to ingratiate himself to her detriment.

To help smooth things over, he'd stopped on his way in and picked up a couple of bagels and two café mochas. His plan was for the two of them to spend the morning strategizing. Under the guise of wanting to compare schedules with Maddie, he'd waited to call Dave back to reschedule. Maybe that would appease her.

Why was he taking such pains to be nice? It was his instinct to call Dave right back, verbally rough him up for canceling at the last minute and then make him feel as if he owed him. That's how business was done.

He went straight to Maddie's office without even stopping by his own. He knew she was there because her white Volvo was parked in its usual spot. Funny how the sight of her car now sparked an instant reaction in him when he saw it.

When he got to her office, her head was bowed as she read something on her desk. It dawned on him that her hair, which she normally wore in a ponytail, was down and covered her profile. Her hair looked shiny and a little bit shorter and fuller. His mouth went dry at the vision of her in bed with him—naked and on top—leaning toward him as he ran his hands through those wild, silky locks, pulling her closer as they rode the wave together—

He cleared his throat and knocked on the door frame with the hand that held the small bag of bagels.

She looked up and smiled at him.

Damn.

She looked…different. Somehow.

The woman who sat in her chair was gorgeous. What was different about her? Her hair, for one. But could a haircut really change a person that much? She looked different to the point that he almost couldn't believe she was the same woman.

"Good morning." He managed to spit the words out. "You changed your hair."

She leaned her face on her chin and flirted with her eyes. "You noticed."

"Yeah. Looks great."

She was in such a good mood, he hated to spoil it with the news that Madison had begged off on their meeting.

"Whatcha got there?" she asked, gesturing to the bag and tray of cups he was carrying.

"Breakfast. Are you hungry?"

"You know me, I can always eat."

She was definitely the same Maddie. But he'd never seen her like this. How had he never noticed how gorgeous she was? It wasn't just the hair.

Or was it?

"You should wear your hair down more often. It looks great."

"Thanks." She reached up and toyed with a piece of her hair.

He'd read in one of the body language books he studied that when a woman played with her hair, it was a tell suggesting she was attracted to the person she was talking to.

The feeling's mutual.

Was it a workplace taboo to comment so much on her appearance? He couldn't help it, and she didn't seem to be taking offense. She'd kissed him...

"I hope you like mochas," he said, as he handed her one of the cups.

"What's not to love. Thanks, but don't you think we'd better take this on the road with us so we're not late for the meeting?"

He slid into the chair across from her desk as she wheeled her chair back and stood up. He noticed the dress she was wearing—the very hot, very pink dress—yes, very hot. It had a flirty little skirt that hit well above her knee and moved when she did. The top of her dress fit her like a glove and even though the neckline wasn't plunging or revealing, it showcased her breasts in a way that had him shifting in his seat.

He took a sip of scalding coffee, burning his mouth and bringing his mind back to the task at hand. There had always been something about her. Something beautifully untouchable that made her feel out of his league and caused him to hang back rather than swoop in as he did with the other women he dated. He'd be smart to stick to business.

"Bad news," he said. "Dave Madison canceled the meeting this morning."

"Very funny." She hitched her handbag up on her arm.

"I'm serious."

The smile that initially suggested she would play along with his prank fell. "You're not kidding?"

Zach shook his head.

Maddie dropped her purse and sank into her office chair. "Why? And when did you find out?"

"This morning," Zach said. "Madison left a message."

She pulled her phone out of her purse and looked at it, then skimmed it onto her desk. "He didn't leave me a message."

"He probably figured I'd let you know."

Maddie *harrumphed*. "Because the two of you are such good buddies. It would've been nice if he could've given me the courtesy of a phone call. Does he want to reschedule?"

"He didn't say." Zach had predicted Maddie wouldn't receive the news well. "All he said was he was called out of town yesterday and wouldn't make it back by our meeting. Why don't you call him and reschedule for us? If you want to. I'm not asking you to schedule my appointments."

"I get it." Her face softened. "And I appreciate it. I've been calling him, but I haven't made contact with him. He seems more comfortable communicating through you. I was looking forward to this face-to-face so I could meet him and we could establish a business relationship. He's a hard guy to pin down."

Zach nodded. "That's how he operates. He's good at what he does, builds a solid product, but he marches to his own tune. Be prepared for that."

Maddie picked up her coffee and sipped it. He could see the wheels turning in her head.

"What does your week look like?" she asked.

"Just schedule the meeting as soon as you can and I'll make it work."

"Thanks, Zach. It's a tight week for me because

Schuyler's wedding is on Saturday. I'd planned on going to Austin on Wednesday. I hope he'll be back tomorrow."

Since Schuyler didn't work for Fortunado Real Estate, she'd only invited the people she knew well. At the barbecue where her father had made his big announcement, she'd apologized to Zach for not inviting him and explained that she and Carlo were trying to keep the wedding intimate with just their family and closest friends.

He understood.

Maddie looked down and toyed with the top of her coffee cup. "I owe you an apology," she said. "Since we're coming down to the wire before Kenneth makes his decision on who he's promoting, for a moment, I was thinking ugly thoughts of you. I wondered if the meeting being canceled was some kind of a dirty deal or a double cross to put yourself in better position for the promotion."

She looked up. "Now I know I was wrong. I think I've been wrong about you all along."

He smiled. "I don't operate like that, Maddie. I know this challenge your father has issued has put us in an uncomfortable position, but I don't believe in stepping on people to better myself. Or bettering myself to the detriment of other people."

"I believe you. You operate that way because of what your brother did to you, right?"

Zach shrugged. He didn't like to talk about his past, but for some strange reason, he wasn't annoyed by Maddie bringing it up. It meant she understood him.

"Probably. But it's in the past."

"Have you ever thought of sitting down and talking to him? How long has it been now?"

Zach shrugged again.

"That would be..." His words trailed off. He couldn't recall off the top of his head, because he'd put Rich out of his mind. "I wouldn't know what to say to him. I don't even know how he would receive me if I looked him up."

Despite all his success, all the money he'd earned and saved and invested, family was the one thing money couldn't buy. It was a rare and precious commodity. He was moved by Maddie's commitment to family. She could've easily let this challenge come between her father and her. It could've caused a big rift right before Schuyler's wedding. But Maddie had her head on straight enough to keep that from happening.

Needing to change the subject, he shot her his most mischievous smile. "What other misconceptions have you had about me?"

She returned an equally suggestive—almost naughty—smile. It pierced him in the most delicious way.

"That doesn't matter now," she said. "But I think I still owe you a few *one things*."

"As a matter of fact, you do."

"Even though I really shouldn't have to pay up from the Ping-Pong match because we never finished. But I do have one thing for you now."

He smiled. He could've resorted to the safety of their usual banter, insisting that she'd forfeited the game so he had won fair and square. But who won and who for-feited wasn't important right now. "Do tell."

"One thing you don't know about me is…" Her voice sounded shaky, and she looked uncertain, like she might back out of telling him what she'd planned on saying. But then she took a deep breath. "What you don't know is, I'd love for you to be my plus-one to Schuyler and Carlo's wedding. Will you go with me?"

After Maddie realized she wanted Zach to be her date to the wedding, she'd promptly overthought it and prepared herself for the possibility that he might not want to go.

If that was the case, she'd been prepared to tell him that it was important to Schuyler for her to bring a date, but bringing someone she didn't know well, someone who didn't know her family, might make a statement she didn't want to make. At the very worst it might take some of the attention off Schuyler because her nosy family would be so curious about who she'd brought. Was it a serious relationship? Was Maddie the next bride-to-be? What a headache. So, she'd decided Zach would be the best bet. Plus, she strategized, after work-ing on this project together, if they went to the wedding together they would present a united front to Kenneth, proving that no matter who won the promotion, they could work together for the sake of Fortunado Real Es-tate. Never mind how they'd both declared they would leave Fortunado if they didn't get the job.

As it turned out, she hadn't needed all the reasons

and strategies she'd prepared. Zach had answered her with a simple, "Thanks. I'd love to be your date."

Date.

He'd actually said he would be her *date.*

Maddie had been so breathless and giddy, it had been almost impossible to contain it. So, she'd shooed him from the office saying she had work to do. At the top of her list? The call to Dave Madison.

Her giddiness had been brought back down to earth with a resounding thud when she'd gotten his voice mail. She'd left a message imploring him to meet them the following day—Tuesday. She disconnected with the sinking feeling that her message had just disappeared into the big, black hole that seemed to have swallowed any interest Madison had in partnering with Fortunado.

The next call she'd placed had been to Richard Mc-Carter, Zach's brother. Since Zach was going to be in Austin for the wedding and Rich lived in Austin, Maddie decided it couldn't hurt to let Rich know that Zach would be in the area over the weekend.

Maddie had gotten through to Rich on the first call. She was certain it had been a good sign.

"Hello, Rich, my name is Madeleine Fortunado. Your brother, Zach, is a good friend of mine and I was hoping you had a moment to talk."

She'd been heartened when he'd sounded eager to hear about his brother. Without sharing any details, Maddie had simply relayed that Zach didn't know she was calling, but she was certain he would be willing to talk to him. She gave him Zach's cell number and hung up hoping for the best.

However, when Tuesday had passed and Friday arrived without a call from Dave Madison, Maddie was afraid that Fortunado's opportunity might be slipping through her fingertips.

"Have you heard from Dave Madison?" she asked Zach on Friday morning when he arrived in Austin for the wedding. Maddie had been there since Wednesday playing handmaiden to Schuyler.

"I haven't heard a word from him. I was hoping you had. The guy can be such a flake sometimes. He's creative and busy and he has the attention span of a gnat. I told you he operates on his own schedule. I'm sure he'll get back to us when he's ready."

"I know, but time is ticking," Maddie said. "Do you think he's jacking us around? Maybe he's contracted with someone else? I wish I knew one way or the other so that we can make a plan B for my father. I've been in touch with Blue Circle Portfolio. They're the ones looking at developing that land in the theater district and if we can nail that down, maybe my dad will forgive us for not landing the Paisley."

"Yeah, that's great," Zach said, as he stared at his cell phone.

"Well, it wouldn't really be great," Maddie said. "But at least we won't go to my dad empty handed. Maybe he will give us more time to woo Dave. What are you looking at? I get the feeling that you're not all here this morning."

Zach laughed and scrubbed his face with his palms. "Sorry. I'm not really all here. The strangest thing happened." He laughed again. This time Maddie detected an air of disbelief in the sound.

"What is it?" Maddie said. "Everything okay?"

"Uh, yeah. Maybe. I don't really know. My brother called me last night. I haven't heard from the guy in more than a decade and he called me out of the blue the night before I'm supposed to be in Austin. You wouldn't know anything about that, would you?"

Maddie turned her attention to her cup of coffee. *"Maay-be."* She winced as she looked up and flashed an apologetic smile at him. "Please don't be mad at me, Zach. I'm only trying to help. I just thought since you were going to be here and he lives here and—"

"It's okay," Zach said. "He sounded…good on the phone. He's eager to talk. We're meeting for lunch today at 12:30. I'll let you know how it goes tonight at the rehearsal dinner."

As Zach steered his BMW into the parking lot of the restaurant where he was meeting his brother, he realized he was nervous.

This didn't have to mean anything. But it could mean everything.

He'd spent his entire adult life pursuing money, romancing his bank account. He'd scored his financial goals. On this side of the conquest, the most important thing he'd learned was all the money in the world couldn't fill the emptiness inside him. Spending time with the Fortunado family, watching their dynamics, seeing how they navigated the sometimes-stormy waters of family relations, made him want the one thing that money couldn't buy.

Granted, he could get married someday and have a family of his own. Lately, when his mind went there, when he started thinking of ditching the lone wolf gig and opening his heart to someone, Maddie was the one his heart kept coming back to. She was fiery and passionate and she had a heart of gold.

If not for her, he wouldn't be sitting here psyching himself up to see his brother—a family member he thought was lost forever.

Zach recognized Rich the moment he walked into the restaurant. His brother had taken a table in the crowded bar area. Zach figured that Rich had chosen that table to cut down on the awkwardness of this first meeting. It was better than being stuck in a corner at a quiet table for two possibly with nothing to say to each other.

When Zach reached the table, Rich shook his hand. "Good to see you, Zach. You're looking well."

Zach returned the pleasantries and they made small talk about the real estate industry and Rich's law practice and his wife and kids until the servers cleared away their lunch plates.

Zach had prepared himself for the lunch to wrap up without a conversation of any emotional depth. Hell, he had gone into this without any expectations. It was the only way to keep from getting hurt. But Rich surprised him when he said, "I don't know when I've ever been as happy to talk to someone as I was when you took my call."

He added, "I'd love to meet your girlfriend, Maddie, someday. She seems pretty remarkable."

Zach didn't correct Rich's use of the word *girlfriend*. And, of course, Maddie was remarkable. She had changed his life in the few weeks that he'd allowed her in. He would be damn lucky to have the privilege to call her his girlfriend.

"I've often thought if I could have one do-over in life, I would go back to when Mom died and I'd do everything completely different. I should have fought for you, Zach."

And just like that, all the walls fell.

"I know I wasn't the easiest kid to deal with," Zach told him. "In fact, I was a pain in the ass. Looking back, I guess I can't blame you for trying to get me into the hands of someone who could rein me in. Since you were my guardian, the police were threatening to put you in jail if I didn't go to school. I was so mad at the world for the lousy hand we'd been dealt, I didn't care about anyone or anything."

"And I don't blame you for hating me even more after you went into foster care."

Zach took a long swallow of his sweet tea, buying time to weigh his words. But he kept coming back to honesty. He and Rich seemed like they were on a good path, but one lunch wasn't going to heal more than fifteen years of estrangement. Unless he said what he needed to say, this reconciliation wouldn't heal them. It would scab over with the truth of his feelings festering inside.

"I'm not going to lie," Zach said. "I hated you for it.

I guess I hated you right up until I realized that your sending me away may have been the formative experience I needed. It's made me who I am today."

It had also made him untrusting and guarded and hesitant to get too close to people because in his experience, he'd found out the only person he could rely on in life was himself. But he was learning to trust. His heart was thawing. Thanks in large part to Maddie and the Fortunado family.

The face-to-face meeting with Rich was a huge step toward embracing the family he wanted. Maybe. Or maybe he shouldn't invest too much of himself too fast until he could see where this was going. They were both older now, both set in their ways and in their routines. Rich had a family—he'd shown Zach pictures, but he hadn't mentioned anything about introductions. He had no idea if he'd even told his wife they were meeting today. But Zach knew he was getting way ahead of himself. He would be content to take today for what it was.

Rich nodded his understanding. "I feel like I owe you something to make up for the tuition I didn't come through with when you needed it."

Zach froze.

Money. It always came back to money. Money ruined everything.

The last time Zach had seen Rich he'd swallowed his pride and asked his brother for help. He'd needed money for college and since Rich was already through law school and building his practice, Zach had reminded him of their mother's wishes for the insurance money. She'd only left the policy in Rich's name because he was the adult at the time. Their mom had thought she was making it easier on her boys that way, that she was keeping their inheritance—as humble as it was—from getting tied up in court where they'd spend more on attorney's fees than the policy was worth. Little did she know she was setting up her sons for estrangement.

Rich hung his head. "When you came around I was going through tough times. I know that isn't an excuse, but it's what was happening."

Rich reached into his shirt pocket and pulled out a fat envelope. "This may be too little too late, because it sounds like you're doing more than all right for yourself, but this is the amount of money that was owed to you. It's cash. So, don't be flashing it around."

Rich laid the envelope on the table. Zach kept his hands folded, afraid that if he touched the money he might turn to stone. He didn't want money. He didn't need it now. It wasn't why he came here.

"And I want to give you something else," his brother added, "to make up for the lost interest. It's something you deserve much more than I do." He pulled out a small black box and pushed it across the table toward Zach.

"What's this?"

"It's Mom's engagement ring. I figure if you ever get around to asking that Maddie to marry you, this might come in handy."

"I told him I didn't want the money," Zach told Maddie in the hotel bar after the rehearsal dinner was over. The story was too involved to get into during dinner. Plus, they'd been seated at long tables and everyone was talking and toasting the bride and groom. It wouldn't have been appropriate to bring up something so personal during the festivities. "But Rich wouldn't take no for an answer. He wouldn't take it back. It's not a lot, but it was cash and he told me to invest it and use it for my kids' college someday when I have kids."

He didn't tell Maddie about Rich giving him their mother's engagement ring, which he'd accepted with no compunction. It was a piece of his mother. All these years he'd never had anything that belonged to her. Even if the ring stayed in a safe-deposit box, at least he would have one thing that had been hers.

"How did you leave things?" Maddie asked.

"We're going to see each other in a couple of months. I may come and play golf. He says he gets to Houston every so often on business. We just left it open. No pressure, but with the feeling that we're going to try. That we both want to try."

"That's great," Maddie said as she sipped her brandy.

"When I first found out you'd called him, I should be honest, I wasn't very happy. But now I can't thank you enough. You gave me back my family."

"I just made the call," she said. "You did the rest. I'm just glad you didn't think I was being too pushy and butting in where I shouldn't."

"Are you kidding?"

Their gazes caught and something sensual and electric passed between them. They were sitting next to each other on a small settee that forced them to sit close enough that he could smell her delicate perfume. She was wearing a wild orange-and-yellow patterned mini-dress that was different from anything he'd ever seen her wear. Come to think of it, other than that tight, hot-pink dress, he couldn't remember the clothes she'd worn in the past. They faded into the background when he envisioned her in his mind's eye. All he saw was her beautiful face and her hair.

She was wearing it down tonight. He ached to reach out and touch it, to run his hands through it and pull her close.

She'd been different since that day she'd asked him to be her plus-one. Or maybe he was seeing her differently. The only thing he knew for sure was that he wanted her.

"I've been thinking about what you said last Sunday when we were in the office."

Maddie squinted at him, racking her brain, as if she was trying to remember what she'd said to him.

"What did I say? I hope I was nice."

He smiled and shrugged, remembering the banter that had led to the crux of what he wanted to say to her tonight.

"You said you didn't mean to be bitchy. And I said I'd never thought of you like that. You're passionate and fiery. That's what I've always noticed about you, Maddie."

He couldn't help himself. He reached out and stroked his thumb over her cheekbone. "I can't help but notice you. You're smart and beautiful. And I think I'm falling for you."

He allowed himself to thread his fingers through her hair. It was as soft and silky as he'd thought it would be. He slid his hand to the nape of her neck and gently urged her into his arms and lowered his mouth to hers. He drank in the sweet taste of her. She tasted like the apples from the Calvados she'd been sipping. The fruit mingled with the taste of the deep, rich coffee that they'd enjoyed after dinner, and there was a hint of cinnamon and spice. He deepened the kiss, needing as little space between them as possible. The feel of her curves pressed against him made him want things he hadn't allowed himself to even think about in a very long time. Not just sex. Not just the physical release that so often came out of the unspoken agreement that long before morning the spell would be broken. Never at his place because he wanted control over the situation. He'd never wanted to open his world to anyone else because it came with too much risk. He'd never wanted to until now. He wanted to take her up to his room and help her out of that sexy little dress and show her exactly how much he wanted her.

Maddie had opened a need in him that was so great it was nearly all-consuming.

"Come with me," she whispered. "I want to show you something."

Of course he followed. He would've followed her anywhere.

She led him to the end of one of the old hotel's hallways. She pressed her fingers to her lips. "Shh."

She looked down the hallway before opening a door—an old closet of some sort that was empty and big enough for just the two of them—that he hadn't noticed because the door was covered in the same old-fashioned wallpaper that was on the walls. She tugged him inside and shut the door.

"How did you know about this place?" he asked.

She answered him with a kiss so passionate that it ignited such a strong need in him that it almost overpowered him.

He wasn't sure how long they made out in the closet because he lost all track of time. It could have been hours or moments, but soon it was apparent that all they were going to do was kiss if they stayed there. The space was cozy and not conducive to lifting her up and... Besides, the door didn't lock, and despite how much he wanted her, he didn't want their first time to be like this. He wanted to savor her. He wanted to unwrap her slowly and treat her like the rare and valuable gift she was.

"Let's take this upstairs," he said in her ear. "I want you to stay with me tonight, Maddie."

Zach's hands cupped her bottom and he pulled her in close so that their bodies were flush, curve melting into muscle, muscle supporting curve. It was hard to tell where his body ended and hers began.

He liked it that way and he wanted to explore every inch of her.

Maddie let her head fall back, which pressed her even closer into his erection. He kissed the soft expanse of her neck and was tempted to slip his hands under that short little dress so that he could explore her breasts— Hell, he wanted to get rid of that dress and all the other barriers between them and bury himself in her until she cried out. But that was the need she brought out in him.

Slow down.

"Come up to my room." He kissed her again, hoping she wouldn't refuse. His hands found their way to the hem of her dress and began making a slow migration up the bare skin of her hip, past the thin strap of her thong, to her waist. He pulled back just enough so that his hand could find the underside of her breast.

Breathless, she broke the kiss, but kept her mouth a whisper away from his. "We need to stop."

Stop?

"God, Maddie, you're driving me crazy. I want you. I want you upstairs and in my bed."

"I want you, too. You have no idea how much. But I can't tonight. I promise we will finish what we've started here. But I promised Schuyler I'd stay with her tonight to keep her from sneaking out and seeing Carlo and being relegated to a life of bad luck."

"Bad luck? What are you talking about?" Regretfully, Zach tugged her dress back into place and put his hand on her back, trying to give them some time to cool down before they exited their hideout.

"It's bad luck for the bride and groom to see each other before the ceremony on their wedding day. It's part of my job as maid of honor to ensure my sister's happiness."

He cupped her face with his hands. "So, maid of honor duty calls?" he said between tiny kisses on her lips, her temple, her eyes—purposely avoiding her neck because if he revisited that sensitive area at the base of her ear, it might be the undoing of both of them.

After he delivered her to the hotel's bridal suite, they made out in the hallway.

"We could stay right here," he whispered in her ear. "I could help you stand guard."

Maddie opened her mouth wider and deepened the kiss. Teasing her, he pulled back, giving himself just enough room to say, "If we're out here, Schuyler won't be able to go anywhere."

Maddie laughed, low and sexy, against his mouth. The sound vibrated inside him and stoked the fire even hotter.

Then Schuyler opened the door. "Maddie, is that you? Oh!"

She slammed the door as fast as she'd opened it, calling, "Get a room, you two. But do it tomorrow night, after I'm married, because seeing you two makes me want to go see Carlo."

"I have to go," Maddie told him.

"I wish you didn't."

"Me, too, but we'll have tomorrow. And all day long, we'll know what's going to happen at the end of the night."

She kissed him again.

"If you keep this up, I'm not going to leave."

He took her hands in his and kissed her fingers one by one. "I'd better go. We don't want to have the fate of your sister's marriage on our heads. Sounds like it could cause a whole lot of bad karma."

Maddie laughed. "She would personally deliver that lot of bad karma to us. I guarantee it."

Still holding her hands, Zach took a step back. "Good

night." The words *I love you* were on the tip of his tongue, but he bit them back because they surprised him. Jolted him. But then Maddie smiled her naughty smile and it turned him inside out.

"I probably won't be able to see you until the reception because tomorrow I'll be my sister's keeper. But I'll leave you with this thought. Every time you see me tomorrow, every time you think of me, remember what's going to happen tomorrow night."

She kissed him one more time and turned to let herself inside the suite.

"We may not make it through the reception," he said.

"I hope not." She closed the door, leaving him hot and bothered and counting the hours.

Five minutes later, Zach was unlocking his own hotel room door three floors below the bridal suite when his phone rang. He thought it would be Maddie and pondered the possibility of phone sex as a consolation for having to go their separate ways tonight.

He closed the door and was preparing to ask her what color that thong was that he'd met in the closet tonight. He'd keep it lighthearted and playful. That way it would either get things started or they could laugh about it before they said good-night. But then he saw Dave Madison's name lit up on the LED screen.

Zach muttered an expletive under his breath. Why the hell was Dave Madison calling at this hour?

Zach answered the call. "Madison, it's 1:00 a.m. You'd better have a damn good reason for calling at this hour."

"Dude! I'm in Australia. I'm all messed up on time. I thought it would be late morning there."

"It's not."

"Yeah, I have no idea what the time difference is. I hope I'm not interrupting anything important."

"If something important was happening, you wouldn't be talking to me right now."

"Sorry to hear that. You losing your mojo?"

Tomorrow.

He heard Maddie's voice in his head, remembered the look in her eyes as she blew that final kiss goodnight.

"Why are you calling, Madison? What do you want?"

"Lighten up, dude. I'm calling with good news. I know you're under a deadline. I wanted to let you know I'm making you the exclusive listing agent for the Paisley."

Madison rattled off some terms he required for the deal. Zach countered on some of the more unreasonable ones. Madison easily acquiesced because he knew they were unreasonable but always tried to push the envelope. The guy was always trying to spin a deal in his favor, but he also knew that Zach wouldn't put up with his crap. He also knew that Zach was the best in the business and could sell out the building faster than anyone in Houston.

"I'll run this past my listing partner, Maddie Fortunado, and I'll get back with you first thing tomorrow. Good?"

"Uh, no. I don't know who this Fortunado chick is,

but I'm offering *you* this deal. Not her. You. Exclusively."

"First, she's not a chick. She's a damn good businesswoman. She's part of the Fortunado Real Estate family. That's the brokerage I work for."

He started to say she'd be running the place very soon, but stopped short. The thought surprised even him.

"Yeah, well, she's been annoying the crap out of me with all her phone calls. So—"

Zach uttered another expletive. "If you'd call her back she wouldn't have to keep calling you."

Dave Madison was starting to annoy the crap out of him. Nobody put Maddie down like that and got away with it.

"All right, whatever. My offer stands firm. I'm happy to bring you on board. The chick can bring in buyers, but she's not part of the deal."

By 5:00 p.m., Maddie was wearing the cardinal-red gown Schuyler had chosen for her. The color matched the rest of the bridesmaids, but since she was the maid of honor, the style was different.

Maddie loved her dress. Adored it. The cut flattered her in all the right places. The silky red fabric caressed her skin and made her feel beautiful and sexy. Most of all, she couldn't wait for Zach to take it off her tonight, when they were both finally rewarded for their patience.

She was falling for him. No, past tense. She had fallen for him, and hard.

Maddie was in love with Zach.

She'd talk to her father and make him work out something so that they both could stay. They both brought different strengths to the table. Fortunado needed them both.

In the meantime, she wasn't going to coast on her love for Zach. She was going to keep calling Dave Madison until he finally took her call. Zach clearly had the advantage since he knew Dave, but he'd stepped back on this, giving her a chance to bring something to the table. Zach had hooked Dave; now she was going to do her part and reel in the Paisley.

Schuyler was in the shower preparing to get ready for the eight o'clock ceremony. That meant Maddie had about fifteen minutes to herself. She fished her phone out of her evening bag and dialed Dave.

To Maddie's utter surprise, just when she thought the call was about to go to voice mail, he picked up on the fourth ring.

"Yeah?" He sounded groggy, as if she'd awakened him from a sound sleep.

"Mr. Madison? Dave? This is Maddie Fortunado—"

The grogginess gave way to a string of expletives that had Maddie holding the phone away from her ear. "I'm in Sydney. You woke me up. What the hell do you want from me?"

Her first inclination was to apologize and tell him she'd call back later. But how in the world was she supposed to know where he was when he couldn't even show her the courtesy of returning her calls—even if it was to tell her he wasn't interested?

"I'm calling about Fortunado Real Estate selling the units in the Paisley. I've left you a number of—"

"I know you have and I haven't called you back for a reason. I've given that contract to Zach McCarter. I'm good here, okay. Stop calling me."

Maddie dropped the phone before she could hang up. It slid under the bed.

As she bent down to fish it out with shaking hands, the full magnitude of Dave's words hit. He'd given the listing to Zach? She'd fallen hook, line and sinker for McCarter's game.

Chapter Nine

Schuyler was a beautiful bride in her mermaid-style gown that hugged her curves, showing them off to their best and flaring out at the knees for a dramatic effect. It was quintessentially Schuyler: sexy and dramatic.

The outdoor wedding had been ethereally romantic in the Mendoza Winery's sculpture garden with its rosebushes and views. The manicured lawn seemed to stretch on for miles, but the area where the ceremony took place, in front of the Spanish-tiled fountain, was adorned with orchids provided by the florist, which enhanced the rose garden that was in full bloom. The flowers, which were lit to perfection, seemed to be at their splendoring best when the couple exchanged their vows under an inky, starry sky.

It was everything Maddie could've wished for her

sister: perfect weather, supportive guests and a loving soul mate in handsome Carlo Mendoza.

It almost made a girl believe in love again.

Well, except for the love part.

Schuyler had found her perfect man, but once again, for Maddie, love had delivered a sharp, poisonous sting.

The mere thought of having to face Zach broke her heart all over again every time she thought about it. That meant the best thing she could do was steer clear of him for as long as possible. All she needed to do was stick it out until the end of the reception and she could drive back to Houston tonight.

Since she was part of the wedding party, it had been easy for her to avoid Zach until the reception. Now that the ceremony was over, the photos were shot and the bridal party and newlyweds had been introduced, it would take some skillful maneuvering to circumvent him without creating a scene.

She wouldn't cause a scene.

He was the last person on earth she wanted to see right now, but she wouldn't ruin her sister's otherwise perfect night.

As the caterers buzzed around with the passed hors d'oeuvres, Maddie saw her father, but, to her relief, there was no sign of Zach.

"Hi, Dad," she said as enthusiastically as she could muster.

"Madeleine, light of my life and apple of my eye. You look beautiful. How are you, honey?"

It wasn't the same cautious, tentative *how are you* subtext: how is the business arrangement going? It was a genuine greeting from a man who was genuinely happy to be celebrating his daughter's wedding day.

"Couldn't be better," she said.

Liar.

"I'm glad to hear that," he said. "Me, too. Lovely wedding, isn't it? You girls did a great job putting this little shindig together."

She knew he was in a good mood because he didn't even joke about how much the *little shindig* was setting him back. She half expected him to make a crack about having to call off retirement to pay the wedding bills, but he didn't.

Instead, when a waiter came by with a tray of champagne, Kenneth snagged two flutes off the tray and handed one to Maddie.

"Thank you, Dad."

"I take it that you and Zach are getting along well," he said. "Isn't he your date? Where is he?"

Maddie groaned inwardly.

Here we go.

No. We're not going to talk about this right now.

"I don't know where he is."

I don't care. As long as you're here and he doesn't appear to be in this ballroom, I don't care where he is or what he's doing.

"I was pleased when Schuyler mentioned that you two might be getting close."

Maddie choked on her drink. "She said what?"

"She mentioned that romance might be in the air. I must say, I approve. Zach McCarter is son-in-law material."

Oh, no, he is not. He is a backstabbing, double-crossing turd.

Never in her entire life had she ever talked about romance with her father. And she didn't plan to start now. He was so very off base about this one. She hated to pull out the big guns, but she needed to put a hard stop to this conversation.

"Speaking of sons-in-law, now that Schuyler is married to Carlo, I guess it will be more difficult to keep our possible connection to the Fortunes quiet for much longer since the Fortunes and Mendozas seem to be inextricably intertwined."

Her father frowned, all traces of the earlier good humor vanishing from his face.

Welcome to my world, Dad.

"My feelings about the Fortunes remain the same. I am still not interested in fostering a relationship with them and I am not encouraging our family to reach out to them. Maddie, you know I've never been fully convinced of the connection. Your grandmother changed our last name when I was a young child. Her name was Mary Johnson. She changed our last name to Fortunado because it was a form of the name she believed we deserved but couldn't claim. That's how we ended up with the Fortunado moniker. Even so, we're Johnsons, not Fortunes. But let's just suppose by some crackpot shot we were related—that Schuyler's right when she suggests that Gerald Robinson and I share the same father, Julius Fortune. The dad, Julius, has been dead a long time.

"Even if it was true, I don't see any benefit in pursuing the connection. From all accounts, I've heard Gerald Robinson—or Jerome Fortune, or whatever his name is—is a cold, hard, cheating SOB. I don't even want to meet him. Why in the world would I claim him as family? Let's leave well enough alone."

"I think that's a great idea, Dad." Maddie gestured to Barbara, who was walking their way. "I think Mom's looking for you."

Kenneth brightened. "Oh, yes, of course. You have a lovely night, Madeleine. Don't worry. Your day to be a bride will come. Hopefully, very soon?"

Maddie kept her expression neutral. It had been a harsh means of stopping the Zach talk, but it had done the trick. Because of that, she was going to let his last comment roll right off her back. She walked over to her three brothers and Lila Clark Fortunado, who were sitting together at a table.

"Hey, guys," Maddie said, pulling out one of the empty chairs.

"Hey, sis." Connor Fortunado stood and hugged Maddie. Since Carlo had so many brothers and cousins, there hadn't been room in the bridal party for her brothers, but, Maddie figured, the upside to that was it gave them more time to talk.

"You're looking good, Mads," said Gavin. "You clean up nicely."

"When did y'all get in?" she asked, aware that Zach had just entered La Viña, the restaurant connected to the Mendoza Winery that was catering the reception.

Gavin had gotten in last night. Having recently returned from their honeymoon, Everett and his new bride, Lila, had flown in this morning.

Against her better judgment, she let her eyes scan the room. She wondered where Zach was. She'd lost sight of him while she was talking to her brothers. Zach was probably spinning another business deal that was bound to make her look bad. It certainly seemed as if he had no interest in anything but business. And that was fine. She wasn't doing business this weekend. She was taking time off to live life, celebrating her sister's marriage.

She laughed at a story Everett and Lila told about their time in Las Vegas, where they'd eloped. As thrilled as she was for her brother, she couldn't stop searching for Zach. She couldn't help but be on her guard. Odd that she hadn't seen him at the reception so far. He seemed to be gone.

So was their father.

"Where's Dad?" she asked.

"He's with Carlo." Everett gestured toward the large window that reached from the hardwood floor to the arched oak-paneled ceiling, offering a breathtaking view of the sculpture gardens. She spotted Carlo and her dad on the winery's lower terrace, enjoying brandy, cigars and deep conversation. The sculpture garden's soft lighting gently illuminated them.

"That looks like a serious talk," Maddie said to Everett. Even though Carlo had taken the old-fashioned approach and asked their father for Schuyler's hand before he proposed, Maddie was certain their father was taking this opportunity to lay down the law, giving Carlo the "you hurt my daughter, I hurt you" talk. She chuckled to herself. If she'd learned nothing more from her parents, it was the importance of family. You might fuss and squabble, but family had your back. Family never double-crossed you. At least not the members of the Fortunado family.

She glanced around for Schuyler, wanting to joke that their father was telling Carlo that now that he'd married Sky, all sales were final. No refunds. No exchanges.

The Fortunado family, she laughed to herself. It was sort of like the mafia without the crime. Now that Carlo had married into the family, there was no getting out. He was one of them for life.

But Carlo was clearly in love with Schuyler. If her dad was having the *scary* talk with him, good-natured Carlo was smiling and nodding and appeared to be humoring Kenneth like a good son-in-law. Carlo had never wanted anything from her father—except his blessing to marry Schuyler. He wasn't interested in the real estate business, as he and his cousins owned the winery and the restaurant where they were right now.

Maybe her dad was right. Maybe the Fortunados had everything they needed in each other. Maybe it wasn't worth the risk to try and merge their family with the enormous Fortune family—or anyone else. When Glammy had been alive, Kenneth used to joke that with the nine of them they had enough to form a baseball team. "Who needs more?" he used to say. But since Glammy was gone and Schuyler had been hot on the scent of proving that Julius Fortune was their grandfather, which would make them related to the Fortunes, their father had been more adamant than ever about closing ranks.

With Carlo as part of the family, they were back up to nine. Actually, since Everett had married Lila, they had their team and a spare. Maybe it was best to leave well enough alone, because when you trusted too easily, sometimes—oftentimes—you got burned.

Maddie felt a pang of envy for Schuyler and Carlo's and Everett and Lila's good fortunes at having found their soul mates.

She hated herself because her gaze unwittingly searched again for Zach. Not in the longing way she had in the past. This time it was out of self-preservation. It was out of keeping your friends close, and keeping your enemies in sight always.

Last night, after that kiss, she'd let herself believe that Zach was her Carlo. She could imagine him asking her father for her hand, promising that he would love and cherish her for the rest of his days…planning a future with her, instead of stealing her future from her.

She watched her father and Carlo shake hands. The satisfied look on her new brother-in-law's face hinted that the talk went well. Her father wasn't hard to get along with. He was a straight shooter who played by the rules and demanded the same from everyone else.

Kenneth had no more than made it inside La Viña when Zach appeared. As if from out of nowhere, he was right there, shaking her father's hand. Kenneth was slapping him on the back in a way that made the anger that had been simmering in the pit of her stomach boil. There was no denying that Zach looked handsome in his tux. The mere sight of him made her melt a little inside in a way that had nothing to do with how mad she was. And that made her furious with herself.

Fantasies were for people who chose to sit on the sidelines and dream. Delusions were for people who allowed themselves to be taken advantage of.

That wasn't going to happen to her again.

Enough with the self-pity. She needed to be proactive and figure out what she was going to do next. She was a strong woman. Strong women didn't play the victim. Strong women didn't make excuses or point fingers. Zach had won. Even if it wasn't fair and square, he'd won, and the sooner she wrapped her mind around it and decided her next move, the better off she'd be.

In the meantime, she wasn't going to sit there and watch Zach McCarter glad-hand her father.

Instead, she grabbed her brother Gavin's hand. "Dance with me."

The band was playing a catchy eighties song and Gavin obliged without hesitation and followed her to the dance floor.

The music was too loud to carry on a conversation while dancing, which made it perfect, because Maddie didn't want to talk. She needed to burn off some of her rage before she did something stupid.

The problem was her father wouldn't see anything wrong with Zach's tactics to secure the Paisley deal. Maddie knew Zach hadn't gone about it honorably or honestly, but he'd sealed the deal when she couldn't even get Dave Madison to return her call. The only way

Dave Madison would go with Fortunado as the exclusive brokerage was if Zach was in charge. That was the bottom line. It was all that mattered.

It was a slap in the face, but the deal was done.

Zach had won.

Plain and simple. She didn't like it. She didn't like the way he did business or the way he'd manipulated her to get what he wanted. Scratch that. She hated herself for allowing him to manipulate her. She'd let her heart get in the way. She'd trusted him when she never should've let him get that close.

"Mind if I cut in?"

Zach was standing on the dance floor tapping Gavin on the shoulder.

"That's okay," she said. "I'm tired and I want to get something to drink."

She walked away and for lack of anywhere else to go, she went to the ladies' room. She couldn't cut out early and go back to the hotel because she was her sister's maid of honor; she still had to make a toast. She needed to be there for her sister until Schuyler and Carlo drove off into the night. That meant she couldn't hang out in the bathroom for the rest of the night either.

She checked her reflection in the mirror, adjusting the neckline of the red gown Schuyler had chosen for her to wear tonight. It was a pretty dress, even if it was bright. The red lipstick she'd purchased that night at the drugstore matched perfectly. Schuyler had informed her that red lipstick was the hardest color to apply because of the hyperpigmentation. It wasn't as noticeable when a lighter color went on crooked or bled outside of the lip line, but red was nearly impossible to mask...without a lip liner and a little bit of practice.

Armed with the proper tools, Maddie had mastered red and looked darn good, if she did say so herself.

And she intended to keep giving herself these pep talks until she felt like herself again.

She was the only one in the ladies' room. So, she looked at herself in the mirror and said, "You can do this. You will get through this. Right now, do it for Schuyler. And soon you will be fine."

She checked her posture and as she pulled open the door, she nearly ran into her friend Billie Pemberton, a real estate agent and family friend who lived in Austin.

"Maddie, hi!" Billie said, as she gave her a quick embrace. "You look gorgeous and the wedding was just beautiful. Schuyler and Carlo seem so happy. They almost make you believe in love, don't they?"

Maddie forced herself to laugh. "I don't know if I'd go that far, but I'm so happy for my sister and Carlo."

"I hear that you and Zach McCarter are an item."

Maddie racked her brain trying to figure out how Billie would know Zach, but everyone in Texas seemed to know Zach. It was a small world and seemed to be getting smaller and smaller as the years flew by.

"We're just friends. This weekend is strictly work-related."

"That's good," Billie said. "He's a good-looking guy, but it would be awkward if you crossed that line—if you know what I mean—and things didn't work out. You know something always happens. Love is so overrated, even the guys who seem perfect wind up disappointing in the end."

"That's the truth," Maddie said. "It was great running into you, Billie. I'm sure I'll see you again before the night is over."

When Maddie stepped out of the ladies' room, the music was loud and thumping. She caught a glimpse of her sister out on the dance floor with Carlo. They looked like they were having the time of their lives and didn't look like they needed Maddie for anything.

She needed some fresh air and decided it was a good time to step outside. She exited the side door and walked down to the sculpture garden where Carlo and Schuyler had been married a few hours earlier.

The event coordinators had removed the Chiavari chairs and the sculpture gardens had been returned to their original splendor. The lush roses perfumed the air and the babbling fountain provided a soundtrack for her senses that eased a bit of the angst she'd been suffering.

And to think, if she hadn't promised Schuyler she'd stay with her last night, she might have taken Zach back to her room.

If she was feeling this bad after just a kiss…

No, she wasn't going to go there.

She walked over to the edge of the gardens, to the place where area gave way to the sweep of green grass that led to the vineyards, and stood there until she began to feel a chill from the cool night air. She crossed her arms and rubbed them, trying to warm up.

"Are you cold?" asked a too-familiar deep voice that

made Maddie's stomach lurch and fall. "Take my jacket. It's chilly out here."

"No thank you," she told Zach. "I was just going inside." Maddie turned to walk away.

"Are you avoiding me tonight?"

"I don't really want to talk to you right now, Zach."

"Maddie, what's the matter? Are you mad at me?"

She stopped and whirled around. "You're really going to stand there and pretend like nothing is wrong?"

Zach stared back at her. "What are you talking about?"

Maddie looked around, making sure they were alone before she quietly lit into him.

"I finally got ahold of Dave Madison. It helps if you catch him when he's sleeping. Either that or he picked up because he thought someone else was calling. Probably that, because he wasn't very thrilled to hear from me. He said he'd already talked to you and the two of you had worked out the details about the Paisley. He informed me that you're going to be handling the listings. Exclusively. Congratulations, Zach. That's quite a coup. What's next? A hostile takeover? Oh, wait, you won't have to because now my father is going to make you the president of Fortunado Real Estate."

She gave him a round of applause.

"It's not as bad as it seems, Maddie. I promise."

"Frankly, Zach, from my vantage point, it couldn't look much worse. When were you planning on telling me? Or were you staging your big reveal to be in front of my father? Oh, wait, that's probably what you were talking to him about earlier."

"Maddie, listen to me—"

"No, Zach, you listen to me. I can't believe you would stoop so low. No, you know what I can't believe? I can't believe that I would fall for somebody who would stoop so low."

She turned around and walked away from him as fast as her stiletto heels would carry her.

"When I was talking to your father earlier, I told him I was withdrawing myself from consideration for the promotion. The job belongs to you, Maddie."

She stopped abruptly, and turned around. "Wait, what? You're withdrawing? What do you plan to do with the Paisley listing? You know you have a noncompete clause. You can't just *take* everything."

"I'm going to stay as long as it takes to sell out the Paisley and then I'm going to marry you, if you'll have me."

She was so angry that her ears were ringing from the blood that had been rushing and the sound of her heartbeat echoing. She thought he'd just said he wanted to marry her. Surely, she was mistaken.

"What did you just say?"

By this time, he'd closed the gap between them and there was no mistaking when he pulled out a small black box from his coat pocket and held it out like an offering.

"I said, I want to marry you if you'll have me. Because I love you."

He opened the box and showed her the small sapphire surrounded by diamonds. "I know it's not big or showy, but it belonged to my mother. When Rich and

I met yesterday, I told him about you and he could tell from looking at me that I was in love with you."

The world was whirling around Maddie, but Zach, standing there holding out that beautiful ring, was clearly, sharply in focus.

"Are you going to say something?" he asked.

Every fiber of her entire being was begging her to say *yes*, to throw her arms around him and kiss him so hard and so long that they would be each other's only source of air. But the practical Maddie, the one who was still feeling compromised, spoke instead.

"But, Zach, what happened with Dave Madison? He made it sound like he didn't want Fortunado, like he only wanted you."

"I handled Dave. I told him without Fortunado, there is no me. But I also realized without you Fortunado wouldn't be the same. At least not for me. I still believe your dad would've given you the promotion in the end, but—"

Maddie smiled. "So, you're withdrawing because you're afraid of losing?"

He smiled back. "You bet I am. I'm afraid of losing you. So, what do you say?" He got down on one knee. "Madeleine Fortunado, will you make me the happiest man in the world and marry me?"

"Yes!" She threw her arms around him and kissed him so hard the rest of the world disappeared.

An hour later, Maddie joined all the other single ladies and lined up inside La Viña for Schuyler's bouquet toss. Even though Maddie was newly engaged, she didn't want to steal Schuyler's thunder by breaking the news at the wedding. She and Zach would wait until Schuyler and Carlo returned from their honeymoon and they'd call the family together and make a big announcement of their own. They'd have to FaceTime her parents since they'd be out to sea on their big cruise. But they already knew. Zach had pulled Kenneth aside and asked his permission to marry his daughter. Then he'd found Barbara and both of her parents had given their resounding blessing.

So, she stood waiting happily for the toss. Before Schuyler threw her flowers, she turned around and looked Maddie in the eyes and mouthed the words, *These are for you.* But when she tossed the bouquet, it split in two.

Maddie caught half and the other part landed right in Billie Pemberton's hands.

"Oh, for God's sake," Billie muttered under her breath, but loud enough for Maddie to hear.

"It's a sign, Billie," Maddie said. "We're next."

"I don't think so," Billie grumbled.

Zach appeared and swept Maddie into his arms. "It's most definitely a sign. Just wait."

Epilogue

The next morning, as Maddie awoke, she kept her eyes closed.

She'd had the best dreams, the sexiest dreams, in which she and Zach had stayed up until the sunrise making love. They couldn't get enough of each other.

A strong arm pulled her in close to his rock-solid, naked body, confirming that what had happened after the wedding was prime-time real life. Her eyes fluttered open and she saw the gorgeous sapphire and diamond ring on her finger.

"For a few seconds, I worried that I'd dreamed everything," she said. "But here you are."

"Here we are," he said. "Let me show you just how real everything was last night."

He entered her gently and they spent the rest of the morning making slow, tender love.

Afterward, as they lay together, tangled and spent, Maddie said, "I want to tell you one thing you don't know about me."

He propped up on his elbow and trailed his thumb over her cheekbone and across her kiss-swollen lower lip. "Tell me something I don't know."

"I love you, Zach McCarter. I've been in love with you from the first moment I saw you. And I don't know if I adequately expressed it but, last night, you made me the happiest woman in the world when you asked me to be your wife. Now I have a surprise for you."

"My love, you are full of surprises."

"While you were catching the garter, I was talking to my father. I suggested that he let both of us run Fortunado Real Estate."

Zach raised his brows.

"Think about it," Maddie said. "You and I bring different strengths to the table. What would be better than us joining forces at work and at home?"

He pulled her tighter into his arms. "It's true, we do complete each other. But we can talk about business later. Right now, I have one thing I want to tell you that you might not know."

"Oh, yeah? What is it?"

"I love you even more right now than I did when you said you'd be my wife."

* * * * *

*Don't miss the next installment of the new
Harlequin Special Edition continuity*
**THE FORTUNES OF TEXAS:
THE RULEBREAKERS**

*Rodeo star Grayson thinks he's finally ready to quit
the circuit and put down roots. Until he meets Re-
altor Billie Pemberton and suddenly, this cowboy is
afraid of how deep he wants those roots to go...*

Look for
FORTUNE'S HOMECOMING
by NEW YORK TIMES *Bestselling Author*
Allison Leigh

On sale June 2018!

COMING NEXT MONTH FROM

H HARLEQUIN®

SPECIAL EDITION

Available May 22, 2018

YOU CAN FIND MORE INFORMATION ON UPCOMING HARLEQUIN® TITLES, FREE EXCERPTS AND MORE AT WWW.HARLEQUIN.COM.

HSECNM0518

SPECIAL EXCERPT FROM

H HARLEQUIN®

SPECIAL EDITION

*Cole Dalton thought letting Vivienne Shuster
plan his wedding—to no one—would work out just
fine for both of them. But now not only are they getting
caught up in a lot of lies, they might just be getting
caught up in each other!*

*Read on for a sneak preview of
the next **MONTANA MAVERICKS** story,
THE MAVERICK'S BRIDAL BARGAIN
by Christy Jeffries.*

"You're engaged?"

"Of course I'm not engaged." Cole visibly shuddered. "I'm not even boyfriend material, let alone husband material."

Confusion quickly replaced her anger and Vivienne could only stutter, "Wh-why?"

"I guess because I have more important things going on in my life right now than to cozy up to some female I'm not interested in and pretend like I give a damn about all this commitment crap."

"No, I mean why would you need to plan a wedding if you're not getting married?"

"You said you need to book another client." He rocked onto the heels of his boots. "Well, I'm your next client."

Vivienne shook her head as if she could jiggle all the scattered pieces of this puzzle into place. "A client who has no intention of getting married?"

"Yes. But it's not like your boss would know the difference."

"She might figure it out when no actual marriage takes place. If you're not boyfriend material, then does that mean you don't have a girlfriend? I mean, who would we say you're marrying?"

Okay, so that first question Vivienne threw in for her own clarification. Even though they hadn't exactly kissed, she needed reassurance that she wasn't lusting over some guy who was off-limits.

"Nope, no need for a girlfriend," he said, and she felt some of her apprehension drain. But then he took a couple of steps closer. "We can make something up, but why would it even need to get that far? Look, you just need to buy yourself some time to bring in more business. So you sign me up or whatever you need to do to get your boss off your back, and then after you bring in some more customers—legitimate ones—my fake fiancée will have cold feet and we'll call it off."

If her eyes squinted any more, they'd be squeezed shut. And then she'd miss his normal teasing smirk telling her that he was only kidding. But his jaw was locked into place and the set of his straight mouth looked dead serious.

Don't miss
THE MAVERICK'S BRIDAL BARGAIN
by Christy Jeffries,
available June 2018 wherever
Harlequin® Special Edition books and ebooks are sold.

www.Harlequin.com

Love Inspired®

Save $1.00

on the purchase of any
Love Inspired® or
Love Inspired® Suspense book.

Available wherever books are sold,
including most bookstores, supermarkets,
drugstores and discount stores.

Save $1.00

on the purchase of any Love Inspired® or Love Inspired® Suspense book.

Coupon valid until July 30, 2018. Redeemable at participating retail outlets in the
U.S. and Canada only. Limit one coupon per customer.

52615678

5 65373 00076 2 (8100)0 12357

USA *TODAY* bestselling author

SHEILA ROBERTS

returns with a brand-new series set on the charming Washington coast.

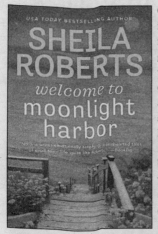

Once happily married, Jenna Jones is about to turn forty, and this year for her birthday—lucky her—she's getting a divorce. She's barely able to support herself and her teenage daughter, but now her deadbeat artist ex is hitting her up for spousal support...and then spending it on his "other" woman. Still, as her mother always says, every storm brings a rainbow. Then, she gets a very unexpected gift from her great-aunt. Aging Aunt Edie is finding it difficult to keep up her business running The Driftwood Inn, so she invites Jenna to come and run the place. The town is a little more run-down than Jenna remembers, but that's nothing compared to the ramshackle state of The Driftwood Inn. But who knows? With the help of her new friends and a couple of handsome citizens, perhaps that rainbow is on the horizon after all.

Available now, wherever books are sold!